TZOQUITO

Dominic Ambrose

Ferrandina Press

Ferrandina Press
New York

https://www.ferrandinapress.com

ISBN: 0615574157
ISBN-13: 978-0615574158

DEDICATION

This novel is dedicated to all those brave people who leave their homes and their families to find a better life somewhere far away in an unknown land.

ACKNOWLEDGMENTS

I would like to thank all of my friends who have given me help and suggestions about this book. I appreciate all of your encouragement. Morphix, Pedro and Lynn in Paris and Fran Gendlin in Mexico, for all your suggestions and technical help; Geri Powder and Toni Ambrose in New Jersey for all your encouragement. I especially want to thank   all of my good friends in the Bayville, NJ, Mexican American community whose journey inspired me to write this book.

A WORD OF CAUTION: The text contains many examples of language that would be considered offensive in English. This was consciously done because I felt that to avoid this would be to create an artificially sanitized version of speech. It is customary in many cultures for young men to teasingly impugn each other's manhood with rude nicknames. As a queer writer myself, I would not want any reader to feel insulted by this. Here, as in many cases, the words are meant to contain no sting beyond the jousting of youth. Perhaps the best indication of this is the unquestioned acceptance by the others of Brolo's barely hidden non-conforming sexual lifestyle.

About Tzoquito and Shape Shifters

The legend of the "binquizac" has been described by the Mexican writer Luis Rosado Vega in his 1938 work, *Amerindmaya*. I have used this concept as a starting off point for the story of Tzoquito. In addition, there are many other legends of shape shifters in Mexican folklore, some of them more familiar. Perhaps the most well known Mexican shape-shifters for North American readers are those found in the writings of Carlos Castaneda.

The cover of this edition of **Tzoquito** shows a famous Olmec sculpture, **Las Limas**. It is made from greenstone and it depicts a human figure holding a were-jaguar baby. Its significance is uncertain. Historians believe that it relates to spiritual journeys, the origins of the human race, or possibly to child sacrifice. Las Limas, thought to be approximately three thousand years old, is an exceptionally well preserved example of the were-jaguar child motif which recurs throughout Olmec culture. It has been used here because the interplay of deity with the half human, half animal child is central to the story. However, it is not known what the were-jaguar represented in ancient cultures, or if the were-jaguar, like the more familiar were-wolf, was able to shift from one state to the other. In another parallel to this story, the statue was stolen in 1970, but then turned up mysteriously abandoned in a motel room in San Antonio, Texas.

Tzoquito
Dogs Descend on Chiapas

1

•

Tzoquito ran down the hill on his strong but unfamiliar legs and rested up against a fat tree. He looked around its trunk. The farm was very close now and he could watch the old man at his morning chores. He had seen this man before. Tzoquito had come down this way in the past, but only at night and only on agile forest legs, as he prowled to the edges of town. On those occasions he had caught mere glimpses of this farmer but that had been enough to let him see that the old man was a gentle creature of the earth. Every thing he did, there in his yard, every one of his movements, looked careful and good. Maybe Tzoquito could ask him for help.

Tzoquito wanted to approach the farmyard unnoticed. He wanted to get closer and introduce himself formally, at close range, though he hadn't quite worked out all the details. Unfortunately, his body wouldn't cooperate - he was not yet used to the big human form that he now possessed, the long dangling arms and the jogging legs and he was too excited to obey caution, so no matter how much he tried to run silently, as he had always been able to do unthinkingly on his soft padded paws, now he made a great thrashing sound through the weeds and tall grass. He himself was too excited to notice but the farmer wasn't.

Don José heard the rustling in the weeds clearly and he turned around to see what the commotion was. The old man saw Tzoquito, this scrawny young man with wild hair, naked to the sun. He saw as he ran hunched up behind the wooden fence and then when the fence ran out, he saw as he dashed behind a bush, then from bush to bush until he got behind the chicken shed.

"Hey! Stop!" said Don José.

Now that the old man was actually speaking to him, Tzoquito lost his nerve. What would he say? He continued to run, in spite of the Spanish talk that the old man was shouting to him. He got to the far end of the shed and stopped for a moment, looking for escape.

"Hey, you! Come here!" Don José went on in Spanish.

Don José hurried to get a closer look, as Tzoquito tried unsuccessfully to hide behind a barrel. Then Don José fixed him with his stare and Tzoquito was trapped, not by any physical tie or rope, but by the penetrating gaze of that old man. So he stayed there crouching, naked, in full view between the barrel and a low wall of boxes stacked against the side of the shed, looking back as one human to another.

Don José approached cautiously.

"Eeeeeh. *¿Quién eres?*" Don Jose asked who he was.

"I don't speak Spanish," Tzoquito answered fearfully in his own Mexican tongue.

"*¿Qué? ¿No hablas español?*"

But Tzoquito just stared back at the foreign words.

"*¿Còmo te llamas?*"

Tzoquito stared at him some more. Don José switched to their common language, the ancient language of this land.

"What's your name?"

"Tzoquito."

Spanish glossary words are printed in italics at their first appearance in the text and they may be found in Tzoquito's Spanish and Mexican Glossary at the back of this volume. In addition, as is customary, Spanish words and expressions not commonly used in English are in italics throughout.

"Where are you from?"

Tzoquito nodded jerking toward the mountain.

"From around here."

"Really? From around here and you don't even speak one word of Spanish?"

Tzoquito shrugged oddly.

"You must be from the hills."

"Yes."

Don José stepped closer, observing Tzoquito's every nervous little move. "Way up in the hills."

Tzoquito stayed put. He was nervous but calming down a bit now that they were speaking Mexican and now that he was finally beginning to say who he was.

"Yes. From the hills."

Don Jose was crouching very low, so as not to tower over him. Now at eye level, he spoke more softly, a kindled fire of interest and compassion coloring his words. "I can see that. One of those hill people from the forest." He was down on all fours now and crawling closer still.

Tzoquito said nothing, looking away and back again. No words were necessary. The old man seemed to know a lot even before he asked. Let him know, rather than ask, Tzoquito thought, for Tzoquito didn't have the words to tell him. No, the shame of his otherliness would be too difficult to admit in words.

"Tzoquito," the old man said and Tzoquito heard his name on a human tongue. "I have never heard that name before."

Don José gave a little knowing laugh and Tzoquito smiled at this kind old man sitting on the earth before him.

"You need some clothes. Stand up, let me see how tall you are."

"Okay," Tzoquito answered, deciding to trust this man. But when the old man got up efficiently to his feet, Tzoquito still didn't move. There were suddenly too many things to think, too many parts to set in motion.

"Come on, stand up! It's alright, Tzoquito. Can't you stand up?"

"Yes, of course I can!" Tzoquito answered proudly, though he was not at all sure that this was true. He held onto the rim of the barrel and got up on his feet, bent forward in an uncomfortable way, like a four legged creature on his hind legs. Don José came up close.

"Here, let me help you," Don Jose said kindly. He took hold of Tzoquito's hand. One human hand nestled inside of another, Tzoquito noted with exquisite wonder. Now his hand was trembling like a pup's paw and he couldn't stop it. Don José was careful not to crowd this wonderful creature, but when he spoke it was as though his mouth were very close to Tzoquito's ear and he whispered in the thinnest of voices, almost not a voice at all.

"Don't worry, Tzoquito. I know who you are."

Tzoquito looked in his eyes as Don Jose continued in this tranquilizing tone.

"I have lived a long time. I've met your kind before. We are all brothers here."

Tzoquito came to life at these words. "Really? Are there others here?"

"Not anymore. A long, long time ago. It's always the same. Young men like yourself. They always come looking for something: a pretty girl, fast talking words, they want to ride in a car, they want to sleep in a Spanish bed."

Tzoquito smiled sheepishly. So he was not the first, after all.

"What do you want here, Tzoquito?"

"I don't know," he answered honestly.

With his free hand, Don José gently pressed his palm into Tzoquito's chest, to make him straighten up.

"There, slowly, slowly, up. Why did you come down from the forest, then?"

"I'm curious, that's all. They call me Tzoquito the curious."

He slowly raised himself to a fully erect position. Now he looked out at the horizon, marveling at the beauty of the earth, as seen from down here in the valley, practically sitting on the earth's belly, practically nursing at its tit. Don José looked across the land along with him.

"Now you can go wherever you like. On two legs!"

Tzoquito looked down and his eyes widened. "The ground looks so far away!"

Don José laughed. "What, far away? It's right there under your own two feet! Come on, come into the house, we will find some clothes for you and *Abuelita* will give you something to eat."

Tzoquito began to walk, looking at the ground.

"No, not like that, Tzoquito. That's how an animal walks, looking at the ground. A man walks with his head up. Looking straight ahead."

Tzoquito looked at Don José and smiled. "A man," he repeated in wonderment. Then he looked ahead at the farmhouse and slowly walked arm in arm with the old man. As they got close to the farmhouse door, Don José shouted out loud.

"Abuelita! Abuelita! Look who we have! Another little brother from the forest! After such a long time!"

Don José's wife came to the door and let a big grin spread out on her face. She was "Abuelita," grandma, because she had had seven or eight grandchildren running around this house in the past. But now, after everyone had gone, on to Mexico City or to Texas on the other side, she was thrilled to have someone to care for. It was not that she was bored or had nothing to do. Abuelita had daily chores to fill all of her time and more: caring for the chickens, growing vegetables and shelling and drying the coffee beans that Don José was harvesting throughout the dry season. But this was a welcome addition. She had given a lifetime of work to the earth and to this mountain forest and now in return, to have it entrust to her care an innocent young brother of the forest, that was something very special.

She took his free hand and ushered him into the house. This was a cool, unusual place where the sun had never shined and he was a bit afraid to enter.

"Come on, my son," she said. "I'll get you a blanket to wrap yourself in, to stop that shivering!"

He pulled the clinging manmade cloth around him and marveled at all the collected objects in the room. He watched as Abuelita fussed around fitting clothes to his height and preparing food. Don

José took him back outside and showed him the farm. There were chickens and two pigs, rows of corn and vegetables and a whole patch of hillside where coffee plants grew in among the trees. The old farmer showed him the tools of the trade, all made of dense metal and dedicated to some one particular purpose. Then there were the baskets, the bins, the sheds, pumps and tubes; all made by men, all ingenious in their specificity.

They returned a while later to the house, where Abuelita served them soup and tortilla. He struggled to eat the soup, but found it deeply satisfying. He felt so comfortable here with these people, that he became very drowsy after that meal and began to nod his head, right there in that uncomfortable human chair.

"Come, I'll set up a hammock for you on the porch," Don José said.

Tzoquito liked the hammock, but would not sleep there, up in the air.

"I think I'll just lay down out in the sun," he said, as he wrapped himself more tightly in the blanket and stepped out into the road. There, in the middle of the driven down dirt, he lay down.

"No, Tzoquito, not there!" Don José said. "Never in the road and not under the sun, either!"

Tzoquito didn't understand about the road, but he obeyed. As for the sun, he could tell that something was odd. "It's strange, the sun is hurting my face," he said with concern.

"Your skin is delicate now," Don José explained. "You will have to get used to the sun little by little."

Get used to the sun? Tzoquito wondered. The sun that he had known every day since the day he was born? But he followed Don José to the shade under a tree, thinking that perhaps the sun was a bit angry about all this and perhaps it was the sun that would have to get used to him. They sat down on the ground and Tzoquito curled up in his blanket and closed his eyes. He hadn't slept much at all the previous night and the exhaustion of all this change was overwhelming him. Or perhaps it was more psychological, the need to close his eyes and withdraw from this great challenging world and return to the world behind his eyelids, his own personal world. He would dream and of course, since he had never been anything but a *binquizac*, a forest creature and knew nothing but the forest, in his dreams he would return to that world, to the home he had left behind.

Thus, with Don José's protective hand laying softly on his shoulder, he surrendered to a deep, enveloping sleep. A sleep that brought him back through all the experiences that had lead him here, to this fateful day.

****

From a high rock, under the blazing sun, Tzoquito could see the whole valley of Cielitos. He contemplated it, with the chin of his hairy snout resting on the hard surface, his furry body curled up on the carved stone. There was Don José's farm way, way down below, with the old farmer just a small dot. The rumbling little town lay beyond. Occasionally he could see movement there, cattle, carts, donkeys and metallic vehicles that would pop out from behind buildings and move about their inscrutable ways.

"Tzoquito!" he could hear his brother calling from the bushes behind him.

He ignored the call. He was Tzoquito, the curious and he was fascinated by the towns. And the stones, too, the ones that hid right here among them in the forest. He had seen so many of these stone carvings that littered the forest floor. What did they mean, these rock-hard faces? It seemed so strange to him that his brother could simply walk by these objects and never ask them what it was that they were trying to say, that he could forage in the bushes steps away from this vista and never sit spellbound by its mysteries.

Tzoquito was not the only curious one, of course. There were others among them and they would exchange stories about the towns or the great stone ruins that they had seen. Some claimed to have even spoken to these stones on the forest floor, or to have walked in those streets in the valley below. It was through this gossip that Tzoquito had heard of a great city not too far away, called *San Cristóbal de las Casas*. For a long time he had begged his father and his older brother to take him there. At last, when Tzoquito had reached his maturity, they agreed.

****

Tzoquito turned in his sleep and wondered if he must awaken and return to some duty or other. Then he felt the reassuring hand of Don José on his shoulder and dimly remembering where he was and who he now was, he decided against awakening. He was not ready and it was not necessary, better to return to that wonderful city, where he had taken his first fateful steps. Thus, he fell further down again, back into sleep, back into the comfort of his past.

****

They had watched San Cristóbal from high on a ridge. Then at night, Tzoquito had snuck down alone to the city and entered the main square, the *zócalo*, a leafy park bordered by fine old buildings. He saw many things in the city: vehicles, stores, great flashing machines. But the most touching experience was when he talked to a group of young people while hidden in the park, among them a beautiful girl named Lupe. The success of this exchange inspired him. He could bridge this secular gap between jungle and the city, between the forest creatures and man. He could do it, he was now sure.

Then in the days that followed that visit, all along the way back to their native mountain above Cielitos, he looked down longingly at hamlets that they passed. On two or three occasions, fortified by the new courage and determination that he had found, he even went to the edge of the settlements near their campsites, but he dared not enter. Nevertheless, even from this distance, he saw marvelous things: lightboxes that spoke and showed pictures, toys of painted wood and string that children swung so skillfully. He had to see more!

By the time they had returned home to their mountain, Tzoquito's thirst for knowledge had become obsessive. Instead of sleeping soundly at night, he spent the dark time sitting on a ridge contemplating the modern world of people. And in the daylight, instead of gathering food to store up or consume that evening, he spent all his days searching the forest floor for signs of the ancient world of knowledge. And so, on one warm afternoon, as he pursued his endless pastime, he found something that would change his life.

There, covered with mulch and clinging stems, was another of those puzzling ancient carvings. Tzoquito exposed a small area before his eyes with three scrapes of a paw. He admired the smooth stone face. He put his cheek to its cool cheek and rubbed his skin there dreaming. He licked the curves and grooves of the sculpture to taste its nourishment. He put his ear to its mouth to hear its words.

But it was silent.

"What have you found this time?"

As usual, his brother's warbling voice startled him...

Tzoquito always expected something entirely different to come from his lips.

"It's an *Olmec* figure. There must be a temple ruin here," he explained, though he knew these things meant nothing to his brother.

"Come, Tzoquito. Don't waste time on old things!"

His brother *Tepiltzin* trotted away on four legs and Tzoquito reluctantly followed.

"Those carvings are useless, Tzoquito. Why else would the many others discard them so?"

"The many others" was what they called the people in the valleys below.

"Come on, Tzoquito! You're too slow!" And once again, as though to pass the time for the long walk back to camp, his brother started the same old lecture.

"Our wise ancestors predicted the devastation that the *conquistadores* would bring. When the many others could fight no more and resigned themselves to share the Earth with these alien people pledged to an alien king, our forefathers took us away to the forests. Here we have remained all these years, far away and free! But it has not been easy, Tzoquito. We have had to develop the cleverness and strength that only forest animals possess. We are *binquizacs* now. The people in the valleys have never understood this."

"Why do they hate us for being binquizacs and why do they call us enchanted dogs, Tepiltzin?"

Naturally, his brother had a ready answer. "They say that we have used the powers of devils to transform ourselves. They have forgotten that neither devils nor gods have magical powers, that the old magic lives only in the memories of the people. Their new language, their new faiths have no words for these memories. They have no idea where magic comes from anymore, so they fear it blindly."

"But with all this magic, do we live any better than our forefathers did?" Tzoquito asked his brother trotting ahead of him, speaking in a tone that betrayed his own skepticism.

"Why should we live better than our forefathers did?" Tepiltzin called back, his voice muffled in the fur of his foreleg.

"Then do we live worse?"

He stopped and turned. "Tzoquito, curious, we do not know how they lived and they do not know how we live. So no one is better and no one is worse. Stop lagging behind and let's go! Papa wants to talk to you."

That was enough to silence the younger brother for a few paces and they trotted on.

Their father had taught them that the many others were unfree, that the many others lived cooped up in the valleys, bumping around each other in their carts, shouting to each other in words they didn't understand. But Tzoquito thought that maybe he was wrong. Perhaps it was them in the shrouded forest that didn't understand, they who lived here banished and alone.

"We say we are free but I am not so sure," Tzoquito said with a defiance that he would never dare repeat in front of his father. "We are confused and confusion is chains. It is as though we started on a journey and have spent so much time learning the ways of the road that we can no longer remember where we were going or what we were planning to do there."

But his words apparently hit deaf ears and Tepiltzin did not respond. So Tzoquito had to content himself with watching his brother's paws hit the ground in broken rhythms as he hurried along. Until Tepiltzin's body folded as he turned to speak.

"Bad day we let you convince us to journey to San Cristóbal!" he grumbled with unusual bitterness. "There is nothing but trouble with Papa ever since."

Now that they were home from that visit, his father was angry and each day angrier and neither he nor his brother knew exactly why. His brother Tepiltzin was moving so quickly through the bushes that Tzoquito was getting dizzy from the pace. What was the great urgency? But when they reached camp and Tzoquito saw his father's frowning face, he knew it would be serious. He began to wonder, could his father read what he was thinking?

"We are leaving tomorrow for the high hills," his father said solemnly.

"No, papa, no," Tzoquito pleaded immediately. "Let's stay here a few more days." He looked down through the trees at the small, peaceful town in the valley below. "I love to look at the village in the dark, when they turn the lights on..."

"Just as you love to rise when we are asleep so you can go visit those forbidden places?" his father said through anger gnarled lips.

Tzoquito didn't answer, just let his head sink lower, hoping to hide his thoughts. Yes, he did love. He loved to gaze at this town like no other town. Because this was Cielitos, the town lived by Lupe, the girl he had spoken to in the park in San Cristóbal. He could not go away. Then with his nose, Tzoquito grazed the smooth pebbles on the ground, the tiniest stones of his ancestors. Yes, even now they whispered to him. Though he still could not decipher their words, these words had a strong effect on him anyway. They gave him courage to speak.

"No, Papa, I can't. I want to stay here."

"This is my decision, Tzoquito. We leave tomorrow."

Then Tzoquito said the words, the words that he could never take back again. The words that changed destiny. "Papa, I am eighteen years old. I have my own rights now, if I choose to take them!"

His brother stared at him in amazement. Yes, of course he had those rights, but to take them... that was irrevocable and the end of their relationship.

"Yes, you have rights, Tzoquito, my son. But be prudent. Don't speak too soon."

"No! I won't be prudent again! I don't want to live like this anymore, live like a dog! I will stay here without you and I will do as I please."

His father came close. "Tzoquito, obey your father."

"No, I am free."

"Tzoquito, obey your father."

"No, I am free."

"Tzoquito, obey your father."

"No, I am free."

And as soon as Tzoquito had pronounced the words three times, the play was complete. He had broken his ties completely. His father moved heavily the last few paces toward him and Tzoquito could see the moisture welling in his father's quickly averted eyes. His father nestled his snout in the fur of Tzoquito's neck. He spoke the final words sadly.

"Then this is goodbye, Tzoquito," the old binquizac whispered. "You are no longer my son."

The father drew himself away and turned his back to leave. His only remaining son, Tepiltzin, looked for a moment questioningly at Tzoquito and then followed the father away through the foliage, leaving Tzoquito there alone, alone between the high hills of his people and the unknown world below.

Suddenly everything sounded louder to Tzoquito, the birds on branches above, the worms in the soil below, even the creaking, pulsing birth of the buds and leaves on the bushes around him, all crowded in on him. He was truly alone now, for the first time in his life. It was a feeling he had felt before when his mother died. But now, there was something new about this loneliness, something greater than regrets. There was the prospect of a future.

He stepped back through the forest, the way that he had come with Tepiltzin. He went slowly, stopping many times along the way to listen to the forest around him in the ways that he wanted to hear it, to smell it as he wanted to smell it. He took so long that by the time he reached that Olmec figure he had discovered earlier in the day, it was already barely visible in the shaded moonlight. He rested his cheek down on that Olmec cheek and he cried. He cried for a loss that he could not explain and for a desire that he could not imagine. He asked the Olmec over and over what he should do, but the figure remained resolutely silent.

And then he slept right where he lay. And dreamed. He was visited there in his dream by an ancient creature, strong and embellished with the finest tattoos and most colorful paint all over his body. This creature held him steady, passing on to him the warmth that came from deep in its stone heart. This creature spoke to him with a startling clarity that quite nearly woke him.

"Tzoquito! You have taken the first step, but one step will not move you until you take the second. And you will never reach anywhere until you walk. Walk, Tzoquito. Walk!"

"But how can I? I don't know how and I don't know where to go."

"Tzoquito, when you were a little child, your mother used to take you to see her brother, the great *shaman Ichtaca*. Do you remember, Tzoquito!"

And Tzoquito remembered, vividly. He had not thought of his uncle for so many years, since the old man had simply gone away and disappeared.

"Your uncle, the shaman Ichtaca, knew many magic things. He knew the parts of fire and the parts of sleep. But greatest of all, he knew the secrets of shifting shape. Do you remember, Tzoquito!"

And Tzoquito remembered, vividly.

"And there was one day, when you wanted the sweet fruit of an apple tree, but you could not get that fruit with your motherless paw. Ichtaca had laughed and said, 'You need a thumb, Tzoquito! You need the mother of your hand!' and he showed you a movement, he taught you a word and he filled your mind with an energy, a force. You concentrated that force, Tzoquito and you made your paw into a human hand, with its thumb and kept it that way long enough to reach that apple and to pluck it from that tree. Do you remember, Tzoquito?"

And suddenly Tzoquito remembered, vividly, something that had happened when he was so very young, something so momentous, how could he have forgotten? But he hadn't really forgotten, for here it was again, alive in every detail in his mind, right down to the feel of that wondrous hand that just for a few wondrous moments had been as human as any ever born of human mother. So precisely, so vividly did he remember, that he shook with excitement and threw himself awake.

He raised his head from the Olmec figure and looked back down at its face – now frozen cold in worldly silence. He looked around in the semi-dark. He could not sleep, he had to think, to go through those memories over and over again. Now he knew what he would do. For that trick that his Uncle Ichtaca had taught him, turning his paw into a hand, had a significance far greater than the ability to pluck an apple from a tree. With that hand he could pluck the humanity right out from deep inside his soul and let it breathe. He wanted to do it immediately, but he could not do it here and now, for the magic needed sunlight and it needed open air. It could not be done in the nighttime forest but only out in the light of day.

The sun appeared as usual that day and like so many other days, Tzoquito was there, wide awake to greet it. Once again, he was at the edge of a ridge, once again he was there above that small town in the valley, Cielitos. But this time it was different. Today he was not returning from a night creeping through the town on all fours. Today he was going there in the light of dawn, he was going there forever.

The legend known by everyone, all the forest creatures, as well as all the people in the valley, was that a human could bring a binquizac back to human form by taking his hand, (or more accurately, his paw) and pulling him out. But this was not so simple: what human would ever touch a binquizac's paw? A binquizac would more likely grow his own human hand than get a real human to touch his own. And, as Tzoquito now appreciated, this was the real value of his uncle's lesson. All night he focused his mind on that trick his uncle had taught him and he tried it over and over again, until he had it right. Then at dawn, when a ray of sunlight glinted through the leaves, he tried it again. And this time it worked! Tzoquito had one beautiful human hand.

That cautious human hand emerged from the low foliage. And next to it, rose the gnarled paw of a binquizac. The hand grabbed hold of the paw and pulled, back and forth the two arms pulled in alternation and with each pull toward the human, the other came more human too.

He felt himself slowly being drawn along. And out. And little by little, he allowed himself to really believe it, that he was becoming human!

A head evolved. It was a young man with long unruly black hair and Native Mexican features. He looked up at the sky and he brought his perfectly lean upper body out above the foliage, naked to the sun. And now it was a chain reaction, something so smooth and natural that it could only have been the fulfillment of mother nature's deepest desire. As each part of his body was touched by sunlight, it was transformed into the smooth and beautiful brown body of a human being.

It was magic but it was also real. He felt the warmth of the sun on his naked skin and just as quickly, the cold air of dawn on my unprotected body.

With a gleeful laugh, Tzoquito rushed down the hillside toward a group of buildings in the valley. He shouted out loud in his Mexican tongue, shouting just as he had never been able to before.

"The sun! My skin! I am free!"

He ran all the way down to the lowland, the floodplain by a small river. There was the farm and there was the old farmer at his chores in the yard. Except that now, when Tzoquito reached the fat tree and pressed his face against its lumpy trunk, he felt the dirt and grass of the ground beneath it, instead. He opened his eyes and realized he had been sleeping right there under that tree and that the sun, now lower in the sky, now milder and finally accepting, was bathing his face warmly in its evening glow. He pulled the blanket up closer around his human form as he sat up and saw the old couple standing before him, with smiles on their faces. He smiled back.

Thus, he came to live with Don José and his wife, the people whose task it would be, as their task had always been, as though appointed by the very stones of this land, to usher the young man into the valley of man.

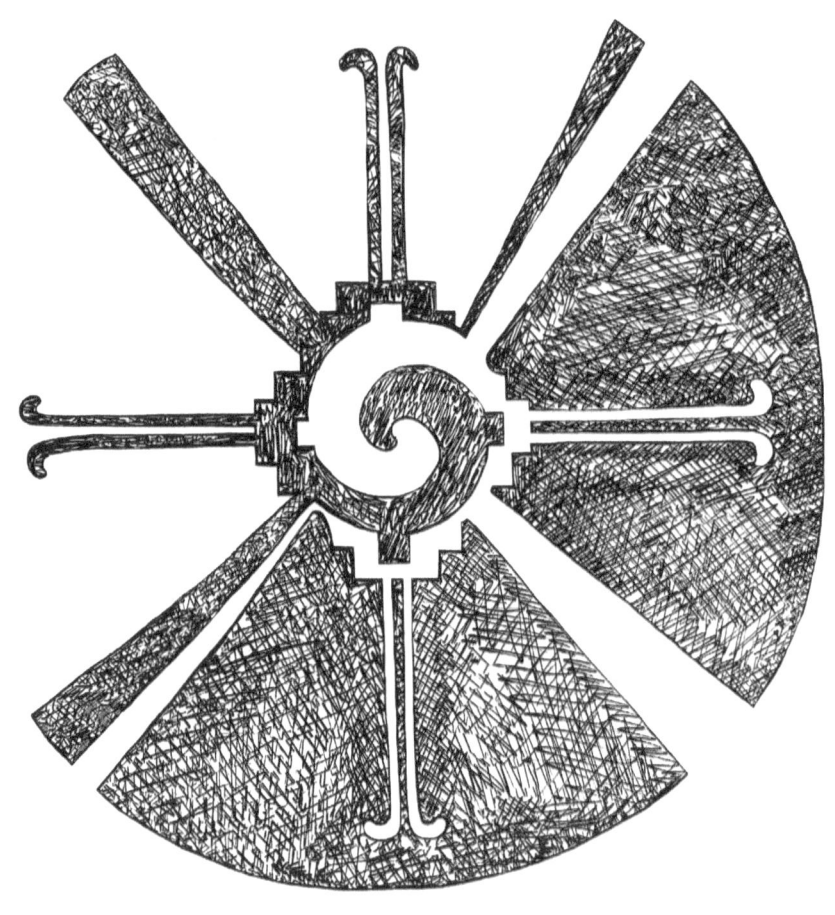

Hunab Ku

2

• •

All the way on the other side of the great land of Mexico, another very different destiny would be moving south, heading straight for Tzoquito. And one evening in that same season as the sun would set, that other destiny would come to a temporary stop in a small town, a nondescript place just north of Ciudad Obregón, *Estado de Sonora.* The town had nothing to recommend it and just about anyone else would have driven right by without thinking twice, but El É, the driver of the big blue Chevy of destiny, had been driving in one shot all the way from Los Angeles and he couldn't drive anymore without some sleep. So that was where the four travelers would have to stay.

They had planned to sleep in the desert but this region was heavily populated and they decided, this once, to find a hotel. They picked the sleaziest place they could find and they checked into the smallest room the guy would give them. After paying their 35 dollars American, they went upstairs to dump the bags that they didn't want to leave in the car overnight.

"Damn, could that room be any smaller?" Brolo, one of the travelers said.

"Yeah," his friend *Jinete* agreed. "Now that we got a room for our baggage, where are we going to sleep?"

"Don't knock it," El É said. "How far do you think a thousand dollars is going to take us on this trip?"

"It's gonna take us to payday!" *Pinto* said, as though rubbing his hands greedily with his words.

"Well, in the meantime, let's be cool. The room is pretty cheap, so let's eat something good. That'll be our one big splurge on the way to *Chiapas*. We spend sixty, seventy dollars in this town, tops. Our money is too important to piss away."

All eyes followed the newcomers as they entered the restaurant and took their seats. First came the leader, El É, the stocky guy with the bald head. He had something to do with the letter "E" judging from the gold chain around his neck with the rhinestone encrusted letter "E" hanging down. Then came his lieutenant, Jinete, a tall skinny guy with a badass limp and an odd pattern on his shaved head. Then the two footsoldiers, Pinto and Brolo. At least, that was how they all saw themselves: leader, lieutenant and footsoldiers, whereas the other patrons in the bar restaurant probably saw something vastly different, something closer to four post adolescents on spring break. There were rude snickers for each of their haircuts and then finally a little rumble of curiosity as Brolo's back came into view. His camouflage hoodie was a size too small, so when he wore the hood up, the jacket rode up in back. That, along with his hang-down dungarees, left a sizable cream colored patch of small-of-the-back flesh and beneath it, a swatch of patterned boxer shorts.

They sat down at a round table and tried to ignore all the curiosity around them. When El É looked over at the barman, he nodded to the menu hanging on the wall, made from plastic letters of varying faded shades of red, clipped onto a board.

"We'll have the *guiso de carne*. It's a casserole for four people, right?" El É said, without consulting anybody.

"I don't think you want that. It has beef in it," the barman said.

"So?"

"Beef is cows, man. I thought you people couldn't eat cows."

"What are you talking about?"

"Didn't you come to see the Swami?"

"Swami? No, man! What Swami?"

"Swami Suchachapati. He came from Los Angeles today, too. He's holding a meeting at the Municipal Auditorium tomorrow, all day."

"Forget that! We're no yogi bears, we're gangstas!" Pinto said.

El É gave him a hard look. Pinto had a way of shouting things out, almost like he had Tourette's and it was embarrassing at times. He was a little guy with a skinny Mohawk shock of bleached hair laying limp with fatigue on top of his head. His pronouncement would have sounded doubtful enough given the visual element, but the squeakiness of his voice made it downright ridiculous.

The barman shrugged and brought the news of an order back to the elderly lady watching television in the kitchen. She broke herself out of a TV trance and ambled over to an ancient refrigerator. Apparently they had missed regular mealtime, at this late hour. No one else was eating, though the place was full of people, nearly all men, leathery, local and drinking.

Seated at the next table was a drunken man with a week's worth of beard. He tapped Brolo on the shoulder with a cane. "If you're really a gangster, where's your ink?"

"Tattoos? I don't have any," Brolo said regretfully.

"Not even on your knuckles? They come out of jail with all these letters on their knuckles, don't they?" He slurred his speech so badly that Brolo had to get his friends to translate it into English. Brolo was born in L.A. and he would have to get used to speaking Spanish full time.

"Yeah, but I've never been in jail. I got caught shoplifting a CD once, but they just made my moms come down to the station and take me home."

"You need a tattoo."

"I've got a tattoo!" El É said, trying to draw attention away from Brolo's dumbass answers. "A totally unique one. Look! An Aztec sun! Nobody's got this."

"My cousin's got that," another man said dryly.

"And that big girl down the street," the barman said to the first man. "What's her name. She's got one, too!"

21

"I see a big patch of girly pink flesh that could use a tattoo, right now!" It was a somewhat unfriendly sounding voice coming from behind Brolo, a section of the restaurant with a flat-out view of Brolo's boxer drawers and a good patch of naked backside. "Maybe a pink rose!"

There were a couple of guffaws. Another voice suggested, "How about Free Parking?"

And another: "Rear Entrance!"

Brolo whispered to El É. "Yo, dude, I'm not feelin' the atmosphere in this place. I don't know if we should be hangin' out here."

"Be cool, man. Anyway, we can't get up and leave now. We already ordered. We'll look like pussies. Just chill out. We're gangstas now!"

They looked up as Jinete's seat got pushed back noisily. Jinete was getting to his feet. He was tall and skinny and stood fairly impressively over the room. He looked around importantly and waited till he had everyone's attention and then he started rolling up his sleeve. Without saying a word, he showed his tattoo to the entire assembly: his big-toothed Quetzalcoatl, the plumed serpent god of the Aztecs. It was multicolored and very well made and had cost his girlfriend a small fortune at the best tattoo parlor in San Pedro. This work of art brought murmurs of admiration. Jinete sat back down, beaming, knowing that his tattoo was a success, but more importantly, that it had trumped El É's Aztec sun, big time.

Finally, there was a sense that they were being accepted. Now, everyone began pulling at their clothes, showing their tattoos: shirt sleeves got rolled up, entire shirts flapped wide open and pant legs flew up. Practically every male in the place, except Brolo and Pinto, had a tattoo. There were some very predictable ones in the most usual places: the barman had a heart with a girl's name in it on his chest, an old man had a blue anchor on his forearm and there were several Lady of Guadalupes of varying quality. There was nothing out of place: no monkeys with buttholes at the bellybutton, or Bart Simpsons or little stick figures with lawn mowers trimming pubes or pits, but as normal as each one was, each had to be presented for review and commentary.

The tattoo show-and-tell went on for quite awhile, too long, in fact and the arrival of their food gave the four "gangstas" from L.A. a welcome excuse to finally ignore the other patrons. They ate for awhile in peace, as everyone else busied themselves buttoning and then re-buttoning correctly between gulps of beer or *bacanora mescal*.

One guy had remained silent throughout the whole show, sitting quietly at the opposite wall, not showing any ink, just staring intensely at the four young men. Then, when they were finishing up their meals, he got up from his seat, gave himself an initial push from the table with one ring bedecked hand and came strutting over on sheer drunken momentum.

The wiry man stopped in front of their table and pushed back his old fashioned derby hat for effect. He announced in English, "I am Porfirio!"

"Well, you don't say," El É replied sarcastically. This place was beginning to annoy him. He was trying to eat.

"I am the arm wrestling champion of the Estado de Sonora!"

"Yeah, well, you get more impressive all the time."

He whipped off his hat and they could see how the rim had creased a line all around his pomaded coal black hair. He came close to El É's face. He had two eyes, one fiercer than the other and a bushy mustache that pointed southeast and southwest, making him look like *Emiliano Zapata*. "Ah, I see, you're a big man in front of the other schoolboys. But you can't be a real gangster if you don't know how to arm wrestle." He looked over at Brolo. "I pick you! With the underwear!"

"Me? I don't do that kiddie stuff," Brolo answered with a laugh to his friends.

"You cannot refuse a challenge! Then you are not a gangster," then came the searing judgment. "You are no *valiente!*"

That got Brolo's attention. "Hey, you don't have to be insulting! I'm up for any challenge, man, but I haven't done that arm wrestling stuff since I was like ten years old."

Porfirio folded his arms forcefully. He wasn't giving an inch. Brolo squirmed under the glare of his eyes.

"What if I lose?" Brolo protested. "I ain't betting money."

"Well, then if you lose, we have to go one step further: to mud wrestling."

"That sounds messy."

"No, it's not. I always wear a raincoat."

Now that was weird and quite possibly obscene, as far as El É could tell. He looked around to see if any ladies were listening to all this. Were there any women in the place? At first they had only seen two older women there, as brassy and local as the men. Now suddenly, he became aware of two pretty young women, who seemed to have appeared out of nowhere. They were walking over and they sat down at the next table and stared meaningfully at the four. Now that they had finished their meal, it seemed that everyone in the bar was going to start fooling with them.

"Where are you from?" one of the girls asked, the one with toasted red hair that had been worked up into a twist at the back of her head. Her name was Carolina.

"Torrance," Jinete said.

"Never heard of it."

"You never heard of Torrance?"

"No."

"It's right by the ocean, sort of like Santa Monica without all the white people," Pinto said.

The girl looked unimpressed by the idea.

"It's practically the Hollywood Riviera!" he insisted. The girls' faces lit up.

"Really? Hollywood? Have you ever seen Brad Pitt around there?" said the second girl, Libertad. She looked like a cat. A calico one, perhaps, given that her hair was a patchwork of several shades of dye.

"Oh, yeah," Pinto said. "All the time!"

"Quit bullshitting, man!" El É said. Don't you see all these girls want is for you to spend money on them?

"Back up a bit, El É," Jinete said. "Yeah, okay, but so what? It's easy for you to criticize, you got a fiancée to go to. Who are we going to?"

"Go wherever you want. But I've been driving for eighteen hours straight. It's eleven o'clock and I'm going to bed," El É said. He took one last look around the room: at the old man singing hoarsely into a microphone at the karaoke, at Brolo arm wrestling with Emiliano Zapata at the opposite wall, at the barman flirting with an older woman at the counter. Then when he was satisfied that he had seen it all and had no desire to see anymore, he got out from that cramped table and went upstairs to their tiny, cramped room full of baggage.

Pinto looked after him. "I bet he's going up now, so he can take the bed."

"Shit," Jinete agreed. "There will hardly be enough room for the rest of us on the floor. That's how cheap he is with our money."

"You're all in the same room?" Libertad asked.

"Damn, we're all in the same bed!" Pinto said. "Four homeys in one single bed!"

"Oh, we have to do something about that!" Carolina said coquettish. She called out to the barman. "Is the big room available?"

"You mean the bridal suite?"

"Yeah."

"And whose going to pay for it?"

The girls nodded at the two post-adolescents at the next table. "Forget it," the barman said with scorn. "You mean the four guys in a single room? These cheapskates aren't going to spring for that. It's ninety dollars a night!"

"What!" Jinete said. But the girl ignored him.

"Oh, don't worry about that! They know Brad Pitt!"

They took the room. It served El É right, right?

Jinete, Pinto and the two girls went upstairs with a full bottle of 92 proof bacanora and playing cards with naked girls on them. Everything went as planned, with all sitting around on the floor playing Twenty One and loosening their clothes in the heat. The girls were fun but squirmy, managing to wiggle out of every move that the two woozy Romeos put on them. But that was okay, because with their pouty grins and giggles, they seemed to make it clear that an eventual rapprochement was in the cards.

That is, until the church tower across the way struck two a.m. That was when the painting of two adoring Nordic newlyweds just about to kiss, which was hanging above the TV set, suddenly caught Carolina's attention. It touched her deeply.

"Oh, my God, that is so beautiful!" she said and then she burst into tears.

"I miss my boyfriend!" The girl wailed. Between sobs and gulps of the last of the bacanora, she proceeded to tell the maudlin tale of her boyfriend's demise. He'd been killed in a motorcycle accident, it seemed. She was now crying and thrashing wide but safely with acrobatic grace. Whenever Jinete or Pinto tried to mumble something sympathetic, she just wailed louder and cut them off.

"I'm sorry," Libertad said to the confused males that lay sprawled, piss drunk in front of her. "When Carolina starts talking about Tony, there's nothing to be done." With that the two girls got up surprisingly steady on their feet, took a pit stop look in the mirror and made a quick exit.

Jinete and Pinto gave each other a disgusted look and with a couple of curse words and a last burst of energy, they stumbled up from the floor and threw themselves onto the bed, where they promptly passed out with their clothes on, spread out across the red shag bedspread, surrounded by dozens of tiny, purse-lipped cupids shooting arrows from the pink wallpaper and doubled by the heart-shaped mirror on the ceiling.

The next morning they went down to the restaurant for breakfast. They found El É there alone.

"What happened to the Sonora playmates?"

"Carolina and Libertad? They had to leave," Jinete said simply. But Pinto, with his big mouth, had to tell the whole embarrassing story.

"Her boyfriend on a motorcycle? Playing chicken with a souped up Grand Am?" El É asked suspiciously.

"Yeah!"

"And his hand-tooled leather boot got caught in the gears? Couldn't get out of the way? I suppose his guts splattered right at her feet."

"Yeah, yeah! How did you know?"

They were singing that *corrido* all night at the karaoke. I could hear it from that tiny room all the way up on the third floor!" El É said. "You got dumped, *güey*!" he laughed, pointing. "They probably get a cut of whatever you spent! It's almost worth the price of that fool bridal suite to see you guys get scammed. How much was it, fifty bucks?"

"Well, with the bar tab, room service and pay-for-porn, a little more," Jinete mumbled.

"Like how much more?"

"A hundred and forty five."

"Shit!" El É shouted and put his head in his hands.

"Don't sweat it, man!" Pinto squeaked. "We're good for it on payday!"

Jinete thought it best to change the subject. "Hey, where's Brolo?"

El É looked up, "I don't know, I thought he was with you guys."

"Really? He didn't sleep in the room with you?"

They looked around at the empty restaurant, at the unoccupied table where they last saw Brolo deep in intense competition with the mustachioed villain. There was no sign of either of them.

"Excuse me," El É called out to the barman, who was right back at work. "Do you know what happened to our friend last night?"

"The one with the underwear? He lost. He went mud wrestling with that weird guy Porfirio."

They took their time at breakfast. They took long showers in the bridal suite. They sat in the narrow lobby watching people straggle by on the street. They waited till the last minute to check out at one in the afternoon. Then they brought all the bags back down to El É's Chevy Impala and sat in the car wondering what to do.

"We could have just called him on his cell," Jinete said darkly, "if you had let us take them along."

"I told you," El É replied, "we are not gonna have anybody tracking us with that electronic shit. We're on serious business!"

"Where could he be?" Pinto said from the back seat. "How long does it take to mud wrestle?"

"Jinete gave him a scorching look. "What were you born yesterday? Maybe someday I should put on a raincoat myself and show you how long it takes." He turned to El É. "That *pendejo* better get back soon, or we should just leave him here to his *lucha libre!*"

They waited some more and now began to wonder and to worry. Maybe this Porfirio was as weird as he looked.

"Maybe we should go to the cops!" Pinto said, but immediately regretted it when he saw the looks that he got. El É went back into the hotel to speak to the barman.

He found him snoozing at the counter. El É shook him awake.

"Hey, wake up, man! What do you work twenty four hours a day?"

"Oh, thanks. No, I'm just working a double shift today, because both Carolina and Libertad called in sick."

El É considered getting upset but then let it drop. That wasn't his nature, anyway, so he got back to the point.

"Where does this pervert Porfirio live? My homey's gone and we need him back!"

"That I can't tell you. But you may find him where you'll find just about everybody else in town today, except me."

"Where?"

"At the municipal auditorium. To see Swami Suchachapati!"

El É came back out, got in behind the wheel and started the car. "Jump in, we're going!" he said.

"And leaving Brolo behind?" Jinete asked with an amused smile, as he slid in beside him.

"No. We're going to find him, at the Swami show. Pinto, go through his bag and find his photo ID from El Camino Community College."

They drove over to the *Yaqui Valley* Auditorium. Obviously, people had come from far and wide this Saturday, because there was a jumble of dented cars and pickup trucks parked everywhere on the sidewalks, the grass and in the plaza. They parked the Chevy all the way across the large plaza on a side street and hurried over.

There was a big canvas sign over the building that said in English and Spanish, "Direct from Los Angeles! Swami Suchachapati, the Hindu master of Destiny!" The front door was open and as they got closer they could hear the insistent murmur of voices inside. It was clear that the place was full of people. They walked up to the two gringo gorillas at the door.

"Invitation?"

"No."

"Contribution?"

"No, we are just looking for our friend. We lost him and we gotta find him fast. Has anybody seen this guy around?" He showed them Brolo's student ID. The first gorilla took a quick look and passed it to the second gorilla. The second gorilla was even quicker and passed it on to a skinny guy further inside and this one didn't even glance at it, but just immediately disappeared with it into the hall.

"Hey, where's he going?"

"He'll show it to the Swami, to see if he'll take your case."

"What?"

"You're not the only people with a problem, you know. People come to the Swami with all kinds of crazy stories."

"What Swami? We're just looking for our friend that's all!" But by now the gorillas were uncommunicative, busying themselves with other more interesting latecomers – ones with money.

So they waited to see what would happen. A minute later, the skinny guy came rushing back through the door with an excited air.

"He'll take you, but it's gotta be right now!"

"Really?" The first gorilla said, eyeing the three stooges with newfound respect. "They must be important."

"Nah, it's because the old lady he put in a trance won't snap out of it, so they're waiting for the paramedics. This will be a good distraction."

The heavyset gorilla stepped to the side, granting them entrance, even without the benefit of a banknote slipped into his palm.

"Go on, get in there. Hurry up!"

The three homeys entered the hall. The place was packed, with standees lining the walls behind all the seats, filling nearly every available space. There was organ music with a few babies crying mixed in, like at a revival meeting. Hanging down at the back of the stage was a huge "om" symbol inside a lotus flower and below that, a Hammond organ where a straw hatted lady sat with her back to the audience, working the keys vigorously, pounding ponderous chords. At the front of the stage was a platform with vases of tall flowers, and in the middle of the raised platform, an exceptionally obese Swami had been artfully placed in a gold cushioned armchair. He was too fat to sit on his crossed legs, so he had merely crossed his ankles on the floor beneath his seat. That was good enough. He wore purple pajama pants and no shirt on his hairless and many layered chest. He had little eyes set in a pasty face and no beard; his only hair being a big fluffy ball of the stuff on top of his head, enough to stuff a pillow. All together, he looked like a chapati bread puffed up with hot air and ready to burst at the first touch.

"Yo, what's with the Swami with the afro?" Pinto asked, far too loud.

"He looks like Fat Albert," Jinete snickered.

"Shhhh!" A congregant hissed at them with a glare. Some high pitched giggling came to them from a few rows away. Jinete and Pinto looked over to see the Sonora playmates, Carolina and Libertad waving at them double time. They grinned big and waved back.

Swami gave a sign to the organ player and the music went soft and full of tremolo. Although Swami Suchachapati made no sign acknowledging the appearance of these new supplicants, he was now definitely occupying himself with their case. He was holding Brolo's photo ID at arm's length in one hand and squinting at it, as though he needed reading glasses. With the other hand, he was pointing to his temple as though indicating to the slowest in the congregation where the work was now taking place. Then he finally looked up and acknowledged the three newcomers.

"What's his name?" he said in English. A little man in a rumpled sharkskin suit stepped up to a microphone at the edge of the stage and repeated the question in Spanish. *"¿Còmo se llama?"*

"Brolo."

"I don't have the answers, my young friends." There was a collective puzzled sigh from the audience. "No, I don't. I am here to empower you. You! I don't have the answer, but you do! You do!" Swami said. His English was peculiar, sort of like Bombay via Baton Rouge. He pointed at them, like Moses in an ancient print. "It is all inside of you! I will transmit my power to you and you will find young Frodo on your own."

"He was just here this morning!" Jinete said.

Swami opened his eyes very wide and scanned the audience expectantly.

"Ah!" The audience murmured with appreciation.

"You see, brothers and sisters? It is working immediately!" he gushed marvelously. Then he boomed to the rafters, in a voice that could be called anything but ethereal. "Such is the power of my thoughts!" He turned back to the three. "He was here, you say? Where, specifically. Concentrate, my son! You can do it!"

"He was here in this town! At the Tres Gallos Hotel!"

The lady smacked the organ keys and "Ah!" the crowd gasped, even louder this time.

"It is amazing, the power, isn't it, my people? Just look at this young man, with the power, he could immediately see the presence of young Frodo! Immediately!"

"What are you fucking talking about?" Pinto shouted.

Swami Suchachapati hesitated for a bare moment, but then continued even louder, "Young Frodo was lost and now he is found!"

"His name is Brolo, and you're nuts!" Pinto was on a roll.

There was an uncomfortable rustle from the crowd and silence from the organ lady. She was at a loss on that one. The Swami handed the photo ID hurriedly to an assistant and waved him away.

"But, oh the devil! But oh, the devil is a jealous fellow, my brothers and sisters!"

Arpeggio.

"And he will put the words of Satan in the young man's mouth. Everyone, push out the devil from the air about us! Push him out! Shout Om!"

"Om!" the crowd shouted over a quick pound of the organ. Swami pointed back at the Om in a lotus.

"I can't hear you! Shout om, my people!"

And the people shouted "Om!" even louder. Organ, too.

"¡No les oigo!" the little man in sharkskin shouted into the mike.

"OOOOOOM!"

Full chord.

"OOOOOOM!"

Full chord. Over and over again.

"This is bullshit!" El É said furiously, "We just got here last night and he went wrestling with Snidely Whiplash and never came back!" But it was pointless, his words were drowned out by the ecstatic "oms" and the newly intensifying riffs on the organ. The assistant arrived with the ID card and Jinete snatched it away and the three friends turned and left, slamming the auditorium door behind them.

At the exit, they were stopped by the gorillas right on the threshold.

"Hey, where do you think you're going? No contribution for the Swami?"

"What, a contribution for that fake? No way!"

"You ungrateful son of a bitch! He took your case, told you where to go to find your stupid fucking friend and you're not giving a contribution?!" He was holding El É fiercely, pulling at the two straps of his wife beater with one enormous hand, while the other gorilla held onto Pinto and Jinete, each with one of his pink porky fists. Thus humiliated, El É saw no way but to concede.

"Okay, okay!"

The gorilla released him just enough to let him pull out his wallet. El É carefully extracted a ten dollar bill from the pad of banknotes there. The gorilla snapped it up and disappeared it into his pocket in one fell swoop of his fat hand, but he didn't seem particularly satisfied.

"Ten dollars? Ten dollars for the Swami's work? That's an insult!"

El É didn't know what to say, but he was saved from saying anything, at least temporarily, by an unexpected interruption. "Hey! El É!" came a voice from outside. Everyone turned to look. There was Brolo waving to him from the sidewalk, next to a grinning Emiliano Zapata.

"Brolo! Let's go!" Pinto said, trying to squirm out of one gorilla's grip and push past the other. It wasn't working. His feet were moving but he was going nowhere.

"That's your friend?" the two fisted gorilla asked.

"Yes!"

"The Swami found your friend!" The skinny guy at the inner door marveled. But rather than sharing in the marvel, the other gorilla at the door was incensed even more than before. Once again he gathered up El É's shirt with his enormous pudgy fingers and rested his knuckles at El É's Adam's apple.

"The Swami Hindu Master of Destiny found your friend and you're trying to get out of here on ten lousy bucks? Are you nuts?" He let go and grabbed El É's wallet and pulled out a one hundred dollar bill. He held it up gracefully in his pudgy fingers so everyone could see how honest he was. "Here," he pushed the now lighter wallet back into El É's chest. "And I'm letting you off easy!"

By now the skinny guy had gone back into the auditorium to proclaim the miraculous news that the Swami's power had brought the long lost Frodo right here to the auditorium. There was a sudden noise of the crowd and a wild up and down glissando on the organ. Now the first of the curious faithful started peeking out from the auditorium.

The gorillas got disoriented by the new commotion and being rather poor at multi-tasking, they forgot about the three punks and let them go. El É, Jinete and Pinto, now mercifully released, ran out to Brolo.

"Where you been, man?"

"I was getting a kickass tattoo, look!" He pulled down his collar and showed where the greasy ink of a new black tattoo took up one whole side of his neck. It looked like an industrial tool of some kind.

"What the hell is that?"

"It's a Mayan Hunab Ku! A yin yang! Or one *chingon* half of it, at least. Porfirio's got the other *chingon* half!"

Porfirio proudly showed them his neck, where a similar tool was on greasy display. "Thank you!" he said to El É.

"What are you thanking me for?" he said.

"Well, we had to ask your wallet for a little loan, while you were sleeping, to pay for the tats," Brolo said. "A hundred bucks, that's a real bargain, you know! And payable on payday, too."

A loud noise of excited people got their attention. They turned and saw that a large crowd was now standing in the doorway of the Yaqui Valley Auditorium, pointing and shouting at them.

"It's a miracle!"

"Come back, come back!"

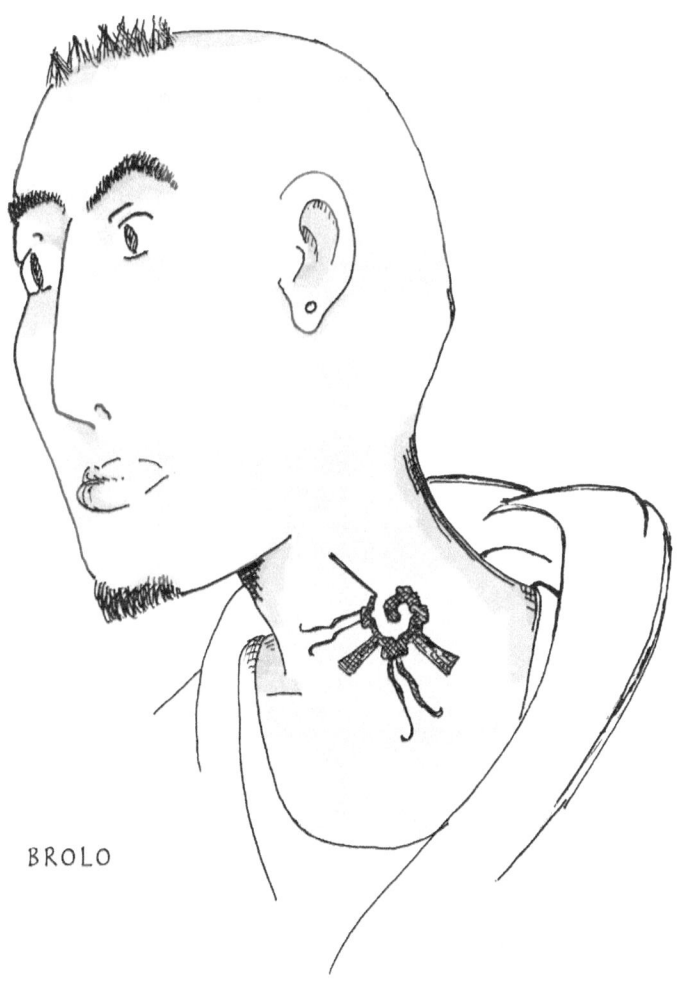

BROLO

"Swami Suchachapati wants you up on the stage to testify!" One of the gorillas came out into the daylight, bounding quickly toward them, apparently on a mission to drag them back inside.

"Come on, let's get out of here!" El É said and three wannabe gangstas began running away across the plaza toward the Chevy.

"Hey, what's the big rush?" Brolo said and Jinete came back and grabbed his arm and pulled him along, too, leaving the baffled Porfirio on his own to face the marveling crowds, the fierce gorillas and the screaming EMS van that had just now arrived to attend to the long forgotten old lady in a trance.

3

• • •

In the days and weeks that followed Tzoquito's arrival at the farm, Abuelita found and sewed clothing for him as he worked in the fields and on the slopes with her husband. In the evening she cooked traditional food that Tzoquito devoured like a wolf. At night, he became accustomed to sleeping on a hammock strung from two poles of the porch. Abuelita kept inviting him to bring his hammock inside, away from the bugs, but he could never do that. The stars were there for him and he would not leave them alone. And the bugs were old friends, too. With the physical labor and the nourishment, his scrawny, weak body gradually had begun to take some form, so he didn't mind sharing some of the largess with these hungry little mosquitoes. The old couple cared for his education, too. They knew what to teach, as this was not the first time they had had this task. They taught him to eat properly at a table, to listen to the radio without howling back at it and to speak words of Spanish.

"The food is soft and so delicious," he said in Mexican and Don José made him repeat it again in Spanish.

"Now you can go back and tell all of them in the forest who makes the best empanadas in this valley, *¿verdad?*" Abuelita added, as though she were ready to civilize the entire population of the forest.

In the mornings, Don José showed Tzoquito how to milk the cow. Over and over again, because every morning Tzoquito would be newly unconvinced.

"Don José, are you sure she doesn't mind giving me her milk?" he said in Spanish, knowing that the cow only understood the most local Mexican.

"What do you think, Tzoquito, she wants to hold it in all day?"

Then several mornings per week they would strap baskets to their waists and walk up into the forested shade and pick glossy red coffee beans from the willing plants that grew there among the trees. At midday, Abuelita would join them with avocados, tomatoes and tortilla and after they had eaten she would return home with a sack of beans strapped to her forehead, as the men continued their work into the sunset.

Tzoquito, like all of his kind, was a phenomenally quick learner and after a few weeks of this, Tzoquito was judged presentable for the neighbors. Don José invited his domino playing buddies to come over one night to see his house guest. It would be Tzoquito's first test.

Tzoquito sat quietly, as the two old men circled around him, inspecting him, as though for head lice or horns.

"What did José say? A nephew from the hills?" one old man said to the other, in strictest Mexican, as though the boy would not understand him that way. "I could see why his sister wanted to get rid of him, he's as dumb as cornmash."

Tzoquito glared at them but they took no notice, continuing to buzz around him like mosquitoes, chatting toothlessly to each other.

"Don José's got a whole tribe of these country cousins, I think," said the little guy with the lumpy skull and a nose like a baby eggplant. "Remember that one, what was his name, Chico, or something? He used to get drunk and howl and laugh all night long in the plaza!"

"Chicahua, yeah, funny name. They called him Chico. Lock your daughters up when he was comin' down the street!"

They both cackled. Then finally satisfied that this one was no odder than the ones that came before, they moved away to get back to their dominoes.

Tzoquito enjoyed the work with Don José. But what he enjoyed perhaps even more, were his evening walks through town. It was with such deep joy that he walked those streets like a man, rather than skulking his way from under car to car, from inside shadow to shadow, like an ugly little enchanted dog. He sat in the little plaza of Cielitos, instead of hiding in its bushes and he walked right down the middle of the narrow streets.

One evening, on the street that curved behind the town's elementary school, he saw something that lifted his heart right to the edge of his skin. He saw two children, Juanita and Miguel and the beautiful Lupe, getting down off the back of an open truck and dragging their bags into a house. There she was, Lupe, the beautiful girl from San Cristóbal.

He went home in a daydream, thinking only about Lupe. At night, during the weeks that he had been here with Don José, he had begun to dream, albeit only vaguely, as a human in this human world. But that evening, as he walked the long way back to Don José's farm, he was transported back to another place and a different body, somewhere that had become so sweet and clean in his mind with the passing of time. With each step along the dark road he stepped further back toward his first meeting with Lupe, the night he had first entered a human town, San Cristóbal de las Casas.

****

Once again, it was that early morning when they had come to the mountainside overlooking the city of San Cristóbal, he, his brother and his father. They spread themselves out supine on the rocks, eating fruit and some meat that they had hunted down along the way. They watched the city through the corners of their eyes, as the people awoke and began their activities, sending blue mists of smoky industry up into the air. They watched for hours, never saying a word, each one straining to feign disinterest as he drank in the view that sated just a bit of his aching curiosity – for even his brother and his father had been enchanted in spite of themselves by the sight of this place. They lay like that all day, until the darkness welled up in the deepest valleys and seeped up through the vegetation like black liquid through absorbent hills. Then they watched as the people lit lights one by one, to continue their rituals into the night.

"These poor people!" Tepiltzin said at last. "All day and night they are condemned to act out the magic of the conquistadores!"

"That is the only magic left to them," their father answered bitterly. "The conquistadores must sit up high somewhere, watching the people turn those wheels of mechanical magic every day, every year, every century!"

But Tzoquito was not convinced that the many others were turning in bondage. Maybe it had started that way, but now it was something else. They themselves in the forest had been transformed, perhaps the townspeople had been transformed as well and like a freefall in a dream that turns finally into lovely flight, their bondage had become freedom. The blue mists of new magic traveled up from below and stung his nose and made his eyes tear, but those people down there were not crying. He so admired their strength.

He closed his eyes and lay still, till he was sure that the others were dreaming. Then he opened his eyes and stretched the sleep away. He looked downhill. Uncountable lights had filled the bowl of the valley blackness; lights far brighter and more beautiful than any that lay in the bowl of the sky above. He curved without making a sound. He would descend to that place and crawl its streets.

At the edge of town, the first few houses were hidden behind high garden walls of adobe and he moved silently through the shadows. Then he crossed the big road and entered where the houses nestled tightly together like the reassembled pieces of an old cracked stone. There streetlights drenched the world in yellow clarity and storefronts with glazing as pure and clear as vertical sheets of still water reflected that light even more. There was no place to hide here and he became afraid. The elders had warned him that the many others would never let a binquizac go unharmed if they ever caught one there. Gathering his courage, he moved forward and immediately hid under a metallic vehicle parked in front of a house. There were many of these vehicles parked alongside the roadway and he slid from under one to the next, progressing this way into the streets of the inner town. From these intoxicatingly perfumed underbellies he saw the townsfolk strolling and speaking in tongues along the blacktop trail.

He marveled at the sculpted feet of the people passing gracefully by. All were snugly fit with soft hide shoeing that protected their tenderness from the hard ground. Only one pair of bare little child's feet came running along and Tzoquito smiled at their merry dance. The toenails were each perfectly formed and they matched each other in two neat rows, like ten curious eyes winking back at him. He could not breathe again until they finally skipped away.

Whenever there was quiet, he moved along, under the next vehicle and the next. He scrambled because he quickly found that some of the glazed buildings reflected his hideous image more clearly than the stillest pond. Soon he was burning with shame for his own ugliness. What would happen if he met a person here? He would scare the lovely creature to death!

He moved from the cars to the long arcades of stucco, running through the blocklong shadows there under the arches. The nestled buildings of the central town seemed to be leading somewhere, to something special. Tzoquito soon found it, when the buildings suddenly opened away and presented a beautiful town plaza of ornate buildings and lush green trees. He hid in the leafy bushes behind the green cast iron benches. He got closer to the seated townsfolk than he had ever imagined possible. He could see them cross their legs and fold their arms with floating grace. They breathed so smoothly and spoke so gently, but not to him. His heart sagged with loneliness.

Many people spoke Spanish, even those that looked as *indio* as the great stone ancestors. Many others spoke a Mexican that he could not understand. Then as he moved along, he saw a trio of young people all dressed in soft white cotton cloth that dazzled his eyes. He approached them and found to his delight that they were speaking a language from some high Chiapas valley, even though they were very far away. They were speaking just like him! They were a miracle, a link between himself and all of this.

There was one older girl who stood facing two children poised on the bench before her, a little boy and girl. Tzoquito tried to understand what she was saying, but although he heard the words, the subject and ideas of her discourse were strange and completely unknowable to him. He was terribly disappointed. He wanted to learn everything from these people, his newfound relatives.

He was shy, he was scared, but above all else, he was Tzoquito. He had to speak. In the mountains they knew how to throw their voices, to confuse the hunted rabbits, so when he spoke, he flung it wide and made it sound as though his voice were coming from everywhere at once.

"Hello, my lady!" he said, suddenly feeling very formal.

The girl swung around, "Who is that?"

"My name is Tzoquito. What is yours, please?"

She giggled. The boy shouted, "It's coming from the loudspeakers!" He pointed at the boxes attached to the trees. So then Tzoquito directed his voice to come from these.

She answered teasingly. "My name is Lupe. From Cielitos. And let me guess. You're Carlos."

"No, I am not. Who is Carlos?"

"Someone who sounds just like you and is the only other person here that speaks like us." She smiled knowingly.

"How are you doing that, Carlos?" the little boy asked. He stood up and looked around. "Where's the microphone?" He squinted and twisted his mouth and said in a mimicking gurgle, "You sound so funny talking through that thing!"

"I'm sorry, I'm not Carlos, but I am your friend anyway. I am Tzoquito. Alright?"

The girls giggled and he was emboldened to continue. "Lupe?"

She looked at the loudspeaker. "Yes?"

"Will you dance for me? Your movements are very graceful and I love to see the people dance..."

"...Please," he said, getting unusual use out of this word.

"No," she said, embarrassed in this very public place.

42

But the ensuing protest from her little companions quickly pushed the willing girl to consent.

"Alright, alright! A little bit!"

She tapped out a rhythm with her fingers and hummed with a quick, delicate tongue. She held her arm high and swung pointy toed about, imagining herself one of those impossibly pretty girls on television at her own sumptuous *quinceañera*.

How was it possible to use the hind legs with such subtle control? He longed to come out from his hiding place and smile before her. It was a foolish thought, for surely she would have screamed and run away. Yet, he yearned to reveal himself, to make the grand confession that had subconsciously brought him to this valley.

Step by step, he was drawn out by his desire to get a better view and to be better seen. The dancer did not notice, intent on her own graceful movements. The littler girl was also unaware, as she studied her elder, perhaps preparing for the day when she too, would cast such a spell. Only the little boy's eyes wandered and they soon locked onto the stranger.

The little boy jumped from his seat like a cub, astonished by this presence. Tzoquito felt a thrill of recognition. He would have loved more than anything to remain there, free before the child's eyes, discovered, confessed and redeemed, but he could see all too well the shock that his hideous appearance had caused in the boy. Instinctively, Tzoquito jumped fast and dove back into the underbrush and lay flat against the dirt. Slowly he looked back up through the stems.

The girl had stopped dancing. "Miguelito, *¿qué te pasa?*" she said in sudden Spanish. "What's the matter?" she returned to the ancient tongue.

The boy stood open-mouth, staring over at the hidden place. The girls saw nothing and were quickly annoyed.

"Come on, Miguelito! Stop fooling around!"

"I... saw a ..... binquizac!"

The word sickened Tzoquito. He burned with shame. The girls laughed. "Oh, really? In the middle of San Cristóbal?"

"Yes! Over there!" He pointed toward the bushes but the girls didn't bother to look.

"There's no such thing!" the little girl said.

"Don't try to scare us, Miguelito. We don't scare so easily!" Lupe scolded.

"But I did!"

"Okay, if you really saw a binquizac, what did it look like?"

Miguelito pondered. "He had furry legs and the head of a boy. He had pointy ears and really sharp eyes."

"Just a stupid dog!" the littler girl scorned.

"No, he didn't look like a dog at all! He looked wild but in a nice way. He looked friendly." The boy looked again toward the hidden stranger. "I liked him!" he concluded.

The words soaked Tzoquito with an unfamiliar warmth. He listened eagerly for the girls' responses.

"Lupe, I'm scared!" said the little girl.

"Don't be silly! There's no such thing as a binquizac. He's making it up!"

"I'm scared anyway!"

Lupe looked around again, sternly this time. "¡*Vámonos!* Let's get out of here!" She took the younger children's hands to begin them on their way.

Their flight threw Tzoquito into sadness. The girls turned their backs immediately as they moved away, unwilling to see anything more. But the little boy moved reluctantly, his head swiveling back toward the hidden creature. His friendliness moved Tzoquito and the binquizac stepped out once again, step by step, until the faint light of a faraway street lamp shone on his glistening fur. The boy smiled and waved goodbye. Tzoquito smiled in return, then ducked back cautiously into the shadows.

Tzoquito lay there for a long time, till there was no one about. Then he scampered back to a parked car to start on his way out of town. He moved slowly at first, waiting under each car for a long time before retreating a few meters more, reluctantly leaving that wonderful plaza in the middle of town, the place where he had met Lupe. But then suddenly he was startled by a quick moving object that scurried up spinning right to him there. It was the gnawed up cob of a roasted corn. He peered back and saw a tall man at the edge of the arcades who had probably just thrown it. Even from this distance it was clear that the man was shaking with anger. And even from here the smell of alcohol stung his sensitive forest nose.

When Tzoquito poked his snout out to get a view, the man fairly jumped with fury and shouted in a language that Tzoquito could just barely understand, but the words were unimportant, the meaning came through crystal clear.

"Get out of here, you filthy dog!" The man picked up a stone and threw it violently at Tzoquito's hiding place. The stone hit a street sign right above him, making a loud crashing noise that frightened the binquizac and made him feel vulnerably visible. He cringed even more at the words that followed. "Go back up in the mountains, *perrito,* where you belong and leave the city to decent people! We don't want your damned country magic here!"

Tzoquito didn't see anything else. He ran away and crossed the big outer road where the cars and buses screeched gigantically around him. He made it out of town in an almost uninterrupted run.

He stopped only when he got back in sight of his sleeping father and brother. He calmed his racing heart a few paces downhill from them and turned to look back at the fast darkening town. He hadn't learned anything about the magic of the conquistadores, but he felt satisfied anyway. He had been scared but that really didn't matter. A boy had called him "nice" and "friendly," words that flushed him with happiness and the boy's parting smile provoked an easy smile of his own for the rest of the night. How had the boy known him so quickly? And the angry man, too, for that matter, in his own hate-filled way? It was not at all true that the memories and the old magic had been irretrievably lost down there in the valley!

But most wonderfully of all, he had spoken to a human of infinite beauty and grace, to the wonderful girl, Lupe.

****

Tzoquito slept especially well that night on Don José's porch and he awoke the next morning with a new feeling, a sense of empowerment. He was human, he was now capable of actually meeting Lupe, speaking to her face to face. Did he have the courage? Of course he did, he thought; he had come this far, hadn't he? Now he couldn't wait to prove it. That day, as they picked bright red

46

coffee beans from the gentle plants, he asked Don José about Juana, Miguel and Lupe. Did he know them? The old man had to think a while, then he realized that Tzoquito was talking about Lino Melendez' children. Yes, he said, he knew them.

"Will you invite them here, to meet us?" Tzoquito asked.

"Do you think you are ready to meet Lupe?" Don José asked. "I think we will have to let Abuelita decide that."

Abuelita gave Tzoquito a few more lessons in table manners and polite talk and in a few days she said that he was ready.

So one evening, when Tzoquito had learned such polite manners suitable for the presence of girls, Lino Meléndez was invited to call with his children at the home of his old friend. So great was the respect that Don José and Abuelita enjoyed in the community, that such an invitation would not be refused.

When Don José and Tzoquito entered from their labors and their washing up, the guests were already seated around the table, being fed by Abuelita. This would be Tzoquito's second big test. By now, Tzoquito was used to Don José's usual neighbors, the coffee farmers. Much of their behavior was surprisingly familiar, so that they seemed just one step removed from the most sophisticated binquizacs of the forest. It wasn't difficult for Tzoquito to relate to them. But these town guests, Lino and his children, were something different. Although Tzoquito knew that they were coming, had known for days, these guests made Tzoquito freeze in his tracks.

Don José slapped hands with his friend, whom he hadn't seen in many months. He touched the heads of the children and with a proud wave of his hand, he invited all to look at his houseguest, who stood fixed to the threshold, as though he were about to bolt right back out again.

"This is my nephew from my sister's village in the mountains. His name is Tzoquito. He lives here with us now."

Now the three children stopped mid bite at the mention of Tzoquito's name. Somehow, this reaction put Tzoquito more at ease. He smiled and said "Hola," but they just stared dumbstruck.

"*Encantada,*" Lupe finally said and nudging the two children, got them to mumble the same.

"¡Encantado!" Tzoquito answered in halting syllables. He smiled and gave a special nod to Miguelito, who smiled back.

"¡Hola, Tzoquito!" the young boy chirped happily.

Don José quickly explained. "When he first got here, he couldn't speak a word of Spanish. Now he is speaking it just like *Hernán Cortés*!"

Tzoquito and Don Jose sat down. Lino looked at Tzoquito with ill concealed contempt. "You didn't know how to speak Spanish? What, they don't have teachers there?"

"Yes, we have teachers but they teach us important things, not Spanish."

"What could be more important than *el castellano?* The language of *Cervantes*?"

"What is that?" Tzoquito asked.

"Who is Cervantes? Just the writer of the greatest novel of all *Hispanidad.*" Now he boomed like a windfilled professor as he announced it: "The story of Sancho Panza and Don Quixote!"

Tzoquito continued eating, unmoved. "Don Coyote? We learned how to speak to coyotes, not to read about them."

"Ah, people in the hills think life is so simple. God bless them!" Lino countered philosophically. "But don't get me wrong. I don't like the big cities, either. I'm glad my children are back home from my sister's house in San Cristóbal. I don't like them staying too long in that big city. They get crazy ideas, like my sister's son, Carlos with his rock and rap and hip and hap. Cielitos is just the right size, right children?"

His children just looked back at him, helplessly. So he continued.

"And, of course, Lupe is glad to be home, because her fiancé is arriving from California tomorrow!"

Don José looked at the young maiden kindly, "Ah, your fiancé!" Then he looked meaningfully back at Tzoquito.

"He's not my fiancé. I haven't seen him since I was ten years old!"

Lino spoke up quickly and settled the misunderstanding. "Her fiancé. It may take her awhile to get used to it, but that is the boy she is going to marry someday." He looked sternly at his daughter. "He was making good money in Los Angeles. Until they threw him out of *el Norte*."

"They threw him out? Why?" Abuelita asked.

"Ah, you know the boys up there. They get bored, they hang around on the street and before you know it, they are getting involved with stupid business."

"With drugs!" Lupe said.

"You don't know that," her father admonished. "You are assuming the worst."

The conversation was beginning to sound like an argument between father and daughter, an argument that had obviously already been played out several times before.

"Anyway, it will be entirely different here, my daughter. There are no bad temptations in Cielitos. His mother says that all he wants to do is settle down here with a nice girl like Lupe and have a family." Lino Melendez leaned in closer to Don José and finished confidentially, if not entirely accurately. "You know, they are the wealthiest family in the whole municipality..." Then as a rueful shadow passed over his face, "... and quite possibly the craziest."

This was the conventional critique and Abuelita would have none of it. "Oh, don't listen to village gossip, Lino. Doña Alba is a very nice lady. Yes, she has some ideas about magic and creatures, but so does everyone around here." She said it with a note of admonition, in solidarity with the young girl Lupe, who seemed to be getting more uncomfortable as the conversation developed.

Lupe jumped up from the table at these words and started gathering up the empty dishes from in front of her little brother and sister and herself. "Time to clear the table!" she declared emphatically. Then she grabbed the still half filled plate from under her father's fork and paused to look at Abuelita. Abuelita motioned her toward the door and Lupe walked out angrily into the sunset. Then Abuelita, too, got up and whisked the plate out from under Don José's fork. Tzoquito managed to rescue his food with both hands before his plate disappeared. He continued eating with his hands, unfazed by the loss of his clumsy fork.

"Wait, *mi hija!*" Abuelita called out shrilly. "I got the rest of them!"

Abuelita went out to join Lupe at the outdoor sink. The two little children and their father stared in fascination as Tzoquito ate his empanada from both hands. Then when he noticed everyone looking at him, he stopped, wondering for a moment what he was doing wrong this time.

"I like the way Abuelita makes empanadas," he said and he went back to biting hungrily.

Lino explained. "Excuse me for staring, but you eat empanadas like you've never eaten before."

"Oh, I've eaten before!" Tzoquito answered and the defensiveness in his voice was momentarily puzzling to all three. Abuelita came back in from outside and rushed over to Tzoquito. She fussed at his face with a towel.

"Ay, Tzoquito, what a mess you made! Go outside, *mi hijo and* wash this sauce off your hands and your face."

Tzoquito was only too happy to obey. It was good enough just to get away from the probing questions of Don Lino, but it was even better for a chance to see Lupe alone. He stepped through the door and stopped on the other side, looking at Lupe. There she was washing the dishes in the sink, moving the plates along, as though performing a dance with her hands. This was the moment he had dreamed of.

She looked up and quickly looked back down at her work.

"I have to wash my hands," Tzoquito explained. He was surprised by his own ease with her. He felt none of the inhibitions that he had feared would hold him back.

Lupe took a closer look and saw his sauce covered hands and face. She gave a little laugh.

"Oh, of course! Go ahead."

She stepped back, but instead of going to the sink, Tzoquito turned away and picked a few leaves from a nearby bush. Then he brought them over to the sink. He rubbed the leaves between his hands under the running water."

"What are you doing?"

"I'm washing my hands."

"But that's not soap you know. Why don't you use some soap? We are not that poor!"

"I know. I just like to do it this way."

Lupe stepped closer and held out a bar of soap to the strange boy. "Here! Rub some of this between your hands."

"I know how to use soap!" he said, too loudly.

"Don't take offense, Tzoquito. I know those country things work too. But I think soap works better. Here!"

He dropped the leaves on the ground and took the soap. He slowly rubbed it between his hands and on his face. And soon he was laughing uncontrollably.

"Why are you laughing?"

"It tickles!"

And for some reason, Lupe had to laugh, too. She stood next to him and went back to washing the plates with a soapy dishrag. He rinsed the soap from his eyes and stared at her as she looked down at her washing. Absentmindedly he continued to rub the soap slowly between his hands, never taking his eyes off of her. She, on the other hand, continued to look at her work. Then she put the dishrag down in the sink and spoke without looking up at him.

"I think you have enough soap now. You can put it down."

He stopped rubbing his hands. She looked up, smiled and took the soap from his hand and he brushed her hand with his. She pulled her hand away quickly, but he remained spellbound, holding his soapy hands out in front of him.

She looks at the hands, then took them, pulling them under the running water. She rubbed them softly, rinsing off the soapsuds.

"Your hands are beautiful, Lupe. And they are softer than the very soap they rinse away.

"Thank you."

She withdrew her hands and gave him a dry dishtowel. He held it out as though he didn't know what to do with it, until she sighed and carefully began to dry his hands and face for him. Now she spoke again.

"You were in San Cristóbal last month, weren't you?" she asked.

"Yes."

"In the park. That night."

"Yes."

"You scared us."

"I'm sorry. Sometimes I don't know what scares people and what doesn't."

"Well, a voice coming out of nowhere. that scares people, Tzoquito. Did Don José tell you to say hello to us?"

"Yes."

"Well, you should have said so, instead of playing a trick. How did you do that, anyway? How did you speak into the loudspeakers?"

"I know how to throw my voice."

"Really? Where did you learn that?"

Tzoquito shrugged. "I don't know. Everyone in my family can do it."

"Miguel got all excited. He thought you were a binquizac. A demon from the forest."

Tzoquito pulled his hands away. "A demon? Why do you call them demons?"

"People say they are demons. That they live in the forest and they do bad things to people out of jealousy."

"Do you really believe that?"

"I don't know. I don't know if they even exist."

"They exist, Lupe. Where I come from, we know that."

"But if they do exist, why do they live up in the forest? Why don't they come down here and live like normal people?"

"I'm sure they would love to live here. But I think they're afraid to. Afraid of everything here, of everything you have." He corrected himself. "Of everything we have."

"I don't know. I can't imagine that they are afraid of us. They live up there among the animals, with nothing at all to help them survive. They must be very brave to do that. What do we have that could scare them?"

"All of this can be very strange, Lupe. All of these cars and machines and big slamming doors. All these people's voices, all this talking, all this crying, all this laughter."

"I don't think laughter is scary, do you?"

"Even laughter can scare you, Lupe. If you can't see it, if you're alone. If you don't understand. I believe those people knew what they wanted when they went up into the forest. They wanted to continue living their lives freely, away from foreign invaders. But once they got there, in the dark, in the jungle, they lost their way, they lost their laughter and now they wander and wander about, just scared of everything."

"I've never thought about that."

"I won't ever be like that, though. I have learned a lot living here with Don José. I won't ever be afraid and nothing will ever be strange, if I hold my head up and look as far ahead as I can. All I need to do is look straight ahead at someplace important, or at someone beautiful and I will know how to reach them. And everything else will be natural and will move into its rightful place."

She was entranced by him and taken into a whirl by the strange and beautiful terrain of his words. He seemed to have access in his mind to a place that she had always just half-glimpsed on the edge of a dream, a certain familiar knowledge that had always eluded her. She was still in that trance as he took her hands and brushed them softly with his. His hands were so oddly gentle, like those of a newborn child. She heard his voice and it was full of a guiltlessness that she had not heard in a long, a very long time.

"When I look at you I know what a person must do," he said, his voice piquant with magic. He leaned forward as to kiss her. That's when she came to her senses and backed away. She pulled her hands from his.

"Oh, Tzoquito! But you don't know what a person must *not* do!"

Tzoquito drew back. "Oh, I'm sorry."

"I'm sorry, too. I am promised to someone else now, I have to remember that. I guess you are right. There are some things here that are scary. Forces. The will of men. They can be very scary, especially when you can't understand them."

Lupe turned back to the sink, back to scrubbing dishes.

4

• • • •

A large, old Chevrolet Impala with California license plates pulled up in front of the Caravel residence, a big modern house at the edge of town. The old Chevrolet was oddly angled, as though it was loose at all its joints and the whirligig sound of its worn fan belt mixed in with the rap music thumping inside, behind the tinted windows.

Some children had run up behind it and were now watching from a safe distance. An old man had stopped in his tracks to stare and a stray dog did the same. The four Chevrolet doors opened and four young men stepped out. El É and Jinete from the front and Brolo and Pinto from the back. They were all dressed almost identically, "gangsta" style.

El É must have just shaved his head this morning; it was as clean as a baby's ass and it made his bushy black eyebrows stand out proudly. He checked to make sure that his rhinestone "E" was hanging perfectly and clearly visible, then he put on a baseball cap and with a forceful thrust, turned it backwards as he looked around at Cielitos.

"Oh, shit," El É said.

A commotion started on the roof of the Caravel home. The sound of a folding chair overturning, of a basket of laundry getting loose and rolling around. And finally, a woman shrieking.

"My baby!" shouted Alba Vasquez de Caravel, as she leaned over the rooftop railing. The driver shaded his eyes and looked up at the partially completed second story and then above that to the gesticulating woman. The other three riders shaded their eyes and did the same, as though mimicking El É's every move. He was obviously a real leader and now he was somebody's baby, too.

"My baby boy!" Doña Alba reiterated.

"*¡Si. Dìme!* What is it?" the El É responded impatiently .

"Egilberto!"

The other three looked at him suddenly, then turned away to hide their snickers. The leader screwed up his face in irritation and turned his hat around to show his mother the Dodger letters "LA" on his cap.

"*¡Ayy, mujer! Me llamo 'El É!'*" My name is "El É!"

However, Alba Vasquez Caravel did not notice the letters and she ignored her son's nickname. She just continued talking excitedly. She spoke to him in Spanish, but he insistently responded to her in English, a language she did not understand. In fact, he spoke these answers down in the vicinity of his friends, as he was evidently really speaking to them and to the entire hick town of Cielitos.

"Egilberto, you've gotten so big, my baby!"

"*Me llamo El É.* And you know I am big! I could take on *Rey Misterio*, one two three!"

"And such a big, gringo car!"

"Yeah and it's all mine now! Let's see those sucka loan officers find it way down here!"

"What's wrong with my eyesight? It looks like magic, like there are four of you!"

"No magic, Mami. *Son mis* homeys. These guys are my homeys."

"Your cloneys? Now how am I going to feed four of your mouths when one of you is already so big and strong?"

"They are not me, mami. These are my friends but you don't have to feed them."

"Thank God! I got scared. They all look just like you, my baby! Just not as handsome."

"Ay, mami, you just don't understand style!"

"Wait right there, my baby! I'm coming down!"

El É shifted his weight uncomfortably. He looked at his three friends, who were equally ill at ease, suddenly finding themselves stuck in this little town of Cielitos, after their disastrous night in Sonora with barely an extra peso between them. And now, the worst fate of all: stuck in somebody else's off-kilter family. But there was one consolation: here, at least, they could be as importantly bad as they wanted. As he waited for his mother to descend, El É crossed his arms "gangsta" style and glared at the old man in the yard across the road. The other three crossed their arms, too and not seeing the old man from their angle, they glared at the stray dog, instead. They had arrived and the show would go on, no matter how pitiful the audience.

Doña Alba, a rather heavyset local resident, came bursting out from the front door. She bounced flat footed and loud down the two front steps and held her breasts in place under her white cotton *huipil* dress as she came running over to her son.

"¡Ayyy! ¡Mi bebè! ¡Mi bebecito!"

She hugged El È forcefully, practically knocking the big boy against his dusty Chevy, in spite of being much shorter than him. She pulled his face down to kiss his forehead.

"But why are you standing around in the street? Come inside and say hello to everybody! *¡Mi bebecito!*"

"¡Ayy, mami!" El É answered with resignation. The others looked away discreetly, as El È was led away docilely by his mother. Then after a few feet, she stopped and looked back at the others. "But what about your clones? Aren't they coming too?"

"No, thank you, señora," Jinete said. "We're going to my aunt's house down the street."

That put a smile of relief on Doña Alba's face, in spite of her hospitality. "Okay," she said and she turned all her attention back to her *bebecito*.

Then when all was quiet again, the three others reached into the car, pulled out their overnight bags and set out down the street, to the home of Jinete's aunt, where they would be staying that night.

On the next morning Doña Alba threw open the front door of the house very early, as though inviting the whole town to come in and celebrate the return of her son Egilberto from el Norte. Inexplicably, no one came. Inside the front room, where Doña Alba busied herself receptively, the bright glare of morning sunlight on the red sheet hanging over the doorway gave everything in the room a pink glow. Then a couple of hours later, the first well wisher: the shadow of a figure came up to the sheet. The shadow put its hand on the red material and moved it slightly to the side. It was Lupe. She poked her head inside.

"¡Hola! Buenos Días! Doña Alba!" she called into the darkness.

Doña Alba came hurrying over to usher her in. Doña Alba was wearing a multilayered huipil frock with elaborate bead and lace embroidery at the top and colorful bands below. It was the finest traditional outfit that she owned. It was her *terno de lujo,* her festival dress and it looked completely out of place on this workday morning.

"Oh, Lupe! Come in, *mi hija!*"

Lupe entered. She was carrying a metal pail. "Good morning. My father sent me over with these vegetables from our garden."

"Yes, I know! I mean, what a surprise!" Doña Alba answered in a fluster. "Thank you! Sit down, my dear, sit down! You should feel at home in this house! Don't worry about helping out in the kitchen, there's time for everything!"

"Thank you."

"And now I have a surprise for you!" Doña Alba said as she unpacked the vegetables from the pail and gathered them in her apron.

"Yes, I know." Lupe answered nervously.

"Guess who came home yesterday? *¡Mi Egilberto!* And the first thing he wants to do is to see you!"

"Oh."

"Egilberto! Egilberto!" the mother shouted.

"¿Qué?" came her son's answer from somewhere inside.

"¡Ven acá! Lupe is here!"

"Who?"

"¡Lupe, mi bebé! Lupe, your fiancée! Ay, you can't hear anything with those music plugs in your ears, can you?"

Doña Alba went rushing out of the room with her arms full of vegetables, in the direction of El É's voice, her own voice trailing off in the distance as she gave him some rambling admonition about diseases that enter through the ears.

Lupe sat immobile for awhile, waiting. Then when many minutes had passed, she got up and started wandering around the room with idle curiosity. She looked at a picture of Egilberto as a little boy, barefoot in the nearby road. Then another picture of El É in Los Angeles, posing fiercely in front of a graffiti covered highway stanchion.

She went over to the opening to the next room, a formal dining room that looked rarely used and she slowly began to move her head around the archway. At the same moment El É's head appeared in the doorway at the opposite wall, just as slowly moving around it to peek at her.

"Oh!" they both said, almost as one.

Lupe stepped back in surprise. Then El É crossed the dining room and entered the front room.

"Hi," EL É said.

"Hi. Welcome home."

"Well, if you can call it that." EL É laughed a bit more at his own witty comment. Lupe looked at him curiously and didn't know how to respond. So he continued. "You know, L.A. is my home now."

"But they said you got thrown out of Los Angeles, right?"

"No, I didn't get thrown out! It was my friends got thrown out. I wanted to leave!"

She knew the real story, everybody did. And she knew he was lying and she didn't like that. So she neglected to catch her words before they came out of her mouth. "Oh. So you wanted to leave and come here?"

"Yeah, I guess so," he said with a sigh.

There was an awkward silence, as they both walked around the room touching things: a funny ceramic monkey with big ears, a set of souvenir plates from Mexico City, a Beauty and the Beast mug from McDonald's. When Lupe made a face at the mug, El É explained. "I sent that to her five years ago."

"I think your mother missed you a lot," Lupe said.

El É shrugged, "That's what happens. People emigrate and life goes on."

"But she missed you growing up. That's a big sacrifice for a mother to make."

"So?" El É answered defensively. "So I was supposed to stay here, just to make her happy? You know she wasn't well enough to take care of me."

Lupe was a bit taken aback by the aggressiveness. It was so unnecessary. But then she realized how much of it was born of shame and she tried to ignore it.

But El É continued in the same tone. "What do you do around here, anyway?"

"I don't know. What do you mean?"

But El É wasn't quite sure what he meant, so he just let himself go. "There is nothing here. How do you expect me to live here?"

"I don't expect anything! I didn't ask you to come back. I didn't ask for a promise. If you don't like it here, then go someplace else!"

"I'm sorry. I didn't mean to insult you," the young man said, suddenly realizing that this was pointless. He came up close to Lupe, seeing the prettiness of her face in the pinkish glow of the room, appreciating her perfect profile, untouched by the harshness of life in Southern California. She turned to look at him, but came face to face with the gaudy letter E hanging around his neck.

She pointed at the costume jewelry. "What is that thing for?"

"That's my name. I'm El É!"

She looked at him quizzically. "What?"

He turned the baseball cap around on his head to show the letters. "El É from L.A.! Not Egilberto. Not at all. *Mi mami* got it all wrong. She hasn't seen me in a lot of years."

Lupe giggled. "That's not a name. That's just a letter!"

"It is too a name! It's my name!" he said, raising his voice a bit too aggressively to the girl.

"Egilberto is a better name than that. E is just a letter, a symbol. Egilberto is a real name!" she said seriously. "It's better than just a stupid letter!"

She didn't know why she was speaking so bitterly, maybe it was his bravado and his impolite style. Maybe it was her need to prove that she wasn't a gold digger trying to make a good catch. Or maybe it was her genuine disappointment. She turned away unhappily. She had liked Egilberto as a child, even had a crush on him for awhile and in spite of her protests, she had harbored real hopes about all this. But now it was clear that her fears had been well-founded. This was not what she wanted in a husband.

"Hey, don't get upset. What's the matter, baby girl? C'mon, look at me."

"Why should I?" she said with fire. "I can't see you, anyway."

"Huh?"

"I can't look into your face. I want to, but I can't. There's too much in the way. All I see is a big silly hat, tattoos and shiny gold necklaces."

"Ah, you'll get used to it. Then you'll see the real me underneath."

"I hope so." She said, trying to be reasonable. But there were too many questions. "Who were those boys you drove up with yesterday?"

"Oh, my *BOYZ! Mis homeys*. You don't know Jinete? His aunt lives down the street. My mother knows her but they're not speaking."

"No, I don't know Jinete and I don't think I want to know any of them. They didn't look very nice."

"They don't have to be nice."

"What are they doing here?"

"Business. You know, regular stuff."

"No, I don't know. Business in Cielitos? What kind of regular stuff? Are they selling drugs?"

El É looked at her with an expression of hurt. "Hey, what are you practicing to be a detective?"

"That's not what I'm practicing to be. Egilberto, I'm practicing to do what my parents tell me I must do. I thought you were coming here to get away from trouble, not to bring it here with you."

"Where do you get these ideas? We got a deal, that's all. Not drugs, but something else. Hey, Lupe, what do you think El È lives on, air? I got here with a lousy two hundred dollars in my pocket. My mother already has it spent three times over. I want to have something too. And any girlfriend of mine would understand that."

"Any girlfriend? How many girlfriends do you have?"

EL É's pride got the better of him and supplied him with an ill-chosen response. "More than enough! Maybe I should have brought one or two with me just to show you what you're competing with."

"What I'm competing with? You can go and call them right now and tell them to come on down and claim their prize. Tell them the competition is over."

"Hey, that's not your decision to make. Don't you have a family to tell you what to do? And now a fiancé too. So why don't you just get used to it."

"I don't need a family to tell me what to do. I've got eyes. I can see and I can hear, El É," she pronounced his name scornfully. "I will know what to do."

Lupe grabbed the empty pail and pushed the red sheet away and walked out into the street. Leaving El É alone in the room, regretting his lack of romantic skills. He pushed over a wooden chair and it crashed to the ground. "Egilberto!" came his mother's voice from a nearby room, well within earshot. "What's the matter, *mi bebé?"*

"It's El É!, mami, El É! El É from L.A.!"

He pushed over another chair and disappeared back into his bedroom.

****

The yard at Jinete's aunt's house was bathed in sunlight. El É and his three homeys were sitting on folding chairs. They spoke in

English; it kept them focused, now especially, way down here in Chiapas so far from the border and almost a week into Mexico.

"Bro, when are we gonna get started?" Jinete said. "We been kicking around Cielitos for three days already." Then he lowered his voice, "And I can't stay at my aunt's house much longer, she's drivin' me crazy. She wants to know everything your mother says. I think she's taking lessons from her on being..." He caught himself when he saw the glare on El É's face. ".... on being strange."

"Yeah and she won't even let me and Brolo sleep in the house, either! I can't sleep on that car seat much longer!" Pinto complained, though everyone could plainly see that he was shrimpy enough to fit easily on its front seat, all stretched out under the steering wheel, if he had to.

"When are we gonna move in on that excavation site in *Tabasco*?" Jinete persisted.

EL É took a few moments to answer. "I don't know." After another pause, he added, "Maybe, I think we should just forget about it."

The three homeys all reacted in unison. *"¡¡¿Qué?!!"*

"What are you talking about, man?" Pinto squeaked. "We came all this way for this one deal."

"I know, man." El É was very uncomfortable in this role, but he had to say it. "But you don't shit where you eat. And this is the last place I got left to eat in."

Jinete was on fire now. He had something of a short fuse. "You gettin' cold feet, man? I don't believe it! Our first chance to make a name for ourselves and you get the fuckin' sniffles!"

"A name." El É said pensively. "What the hell is a name, anyway?" It sounded very uncharacteristic, almost Shakespearean and this made the others worry even more.

In a moment, Pinto continued, "One freakin' deal, El È and we be rollin' in money. We'll be pushin' the chicks to one side, like walkin' into that hen house over there!" He pointed to a particularly dilapidated chicken shed in the next yard.

"What are you goin' on about?" Jinete snapped.

Pinto explained, "Yeah! Only these chicks are the sexy ones."

Now Brolo spoke, his voice emanating from his hoodie sweatshirt, which he wore wrapped around himself in spite of the hot sunlight. "All we got to do is get six or seven boxes of old junk out of that broken-down depot by that river..."

"The *Usumacinta* River," Pinto said, giving his Mexican geography lesson for the day. Brolo was a freeway baby, third generation Angeleno. He had no clue where he was.

"Whatever!" Brolo said impatiently. "Like I said, all we gotta do is bring the boxes out and up to D.F. that's it! It couldn't be easier!"

El É was a leader, he told himself and a leader had to make decisions. So he pressed on. "I guess so, but I'm thinkin' now, about consequences and shit. I'm trying to look to the future, for a change."

Brolo pulled his head out and smiled persuasively. "Well, look at this, Bro. You and us in Mexico City, D.F. We got our money, we got our car, we got nothing left to do but party all night and sleep all day for as far into the future as you wanna see. And when we get sick of that, we just head back to L.A. clean as first graders at Sunday morning church."

He looked guiltily at El È, just then remembering El É's status problem. "Well, we three go back to L.A."

Brolo's momentary lapse made El É stronger in his conviction. Yes, they would all go back to California with their U.S. passports and leave El É behind with the consequences.

"Do you guys know what you're talkin' about? How much money do you think we're gonna get out of this, anyway?"

Brolo had a ready answer. "Enough to send you back here to Cielitos a big man! Just wait till that Lupe sees you then."

"You mean, if she will even look at me then."

Now Pinto was angry, too. "Oh, yeah, that's it. The woman! That's where it always ends. Hey, man, what the hell are you worried about? It's not like we are moving drugs, we're moving some all broken up junk from some old Indian cave. Who wants that old shit anyway except some crazy gringo art dealers?"

EL É hated to say it, but there it was. "But it's stealing. And stealing big time, or else why would they be giving us all that money to get it out? We could go to jail for years for that shit. And it's not right. It's just not right."

Jinete spoke seriously now, sounding like the lieutenant that he claimed to be and something even more. "Listen, man, we're gonna do our deal and we're gonna make our money, whether you are in on it or not. I didn't come all the way to this freakin' Indian reservation just to talk like a born again sinner. You decide, El È, you in or you out. And you decide now, so we can get on with it!"

EL É had to give in. After all, they had come this far. "Okay! Fine. Let's do it!"

Pinto chirped, "Alright!" And when his voice broke like this, all the homeys started laughing with relief, low fives all around.

All except Brolo, whose five finger slap failed to make any contact. His attention had strayed elsewhere. He was looking at something in the distance: a motionless figure sitting halfway up the hillside. It was Tzoquito, sitting hunched up with his chin on his knees, looking downhill in another direction.

"Hey, El È," Brolo said. "Isn't that that crazy little guy you were talking to yesterday? The one who could barely speak Spanish?"

EL É looked and saw the figure on the hillside. "Yeah, I think so. Yeah, that's right. Tzoquito."

At the mention of his name, Tzoquito, turned abruptly to look in their direction.

Pinto laughed. "Oh, shit! He heard you!"

"Get the fuck outta here!" El É laughed back. "How could he hear me from half a mile away?"

Jinete snarled, "Hey, you think that *maricon* is spying on us?"

Brolo calmed him down, as usual. "No, he wasn't even looking over here."

But Pinto was ready to keep it going. "He was facing that direction, those houses. Hey, El È, he's peepin' where your girl Lupe lives!"

Brolo got in the act, pointing at El É. They all laughed, except for El É. They were going to tease him for all it was worth. He had it coming, didn't he, after scaring them so?

"Yeah, man," Jinete said. "I think he got the hots for her. That's where we saw him last night, just hanging around in front of Lupe's house."

"No, he better have more sense than that. I'll be all over his ass, Rey Misterio style, before he knows what hit him." But the bravado couldn't mask the hint of concern in El É's voice. He stood up and shouted in Tzoquito's direction.

"Hey, Tzoquito, *¡ven acá, puto!*"

The disrespectful term struck them all as exceptionally funny, there in the buoyantly relieved atmosphere created by their recent agreement. In any case, the foursome turned their backs on the hillside, laughing to each other some more. Even El É was smiling and joining in, now as they once again laughed like teenagers.

Jinete spoke through his giggles. "Hey, why don't we make an extra box and put him in it to sell to the gringos? He's like some old Indian relic from a cave!"

The others nodded their heads gleefully, but their giggles came to an abrupt halt when they heard a loud thump in the bushes behind them. Although only half a minute had gone by since El É's shout to Tzoquito, the strange *indio* had apparently just vaulted over the high cinderblock garden wall and come crashing down into the yard. The foursome jumped up, startled when they turned and saw him standing awkwardly there behind them.

"*¡Hola!*" Tzoquito said.

"Whoa! How'd you get here so quick?" El É said, switching to Spanish for Tzoquito's benefit.

"I walked," he answered proudly.

"A half a mile in two seconds?" Jinete asked.

"It wasn't two seconds. It was seventeen seconds. Anyway, I can walk fast. When I set my mind to it. All I do is look at where I'm going and I get there."

With the laughter long gone and forgotten, the foursome from California locked back down into gangsta mode. It was good practice and Tzoquito would be an easy stooge. Three homeys eyed Tzoquito hostilely, as El È spoke.

"Yo, Tzoquito. What are you doin', starin' at my girlfriend's house?"

"You mean Lupe?" Tzoquito asked innocently.

"Yo, who the heck you think I mean?"

"Are you sure she's your girlfriend?"

The homeys looked wide-eyed at El É to see his next move. Then they found his reaction just as surprising. "Hey, why do you say that? Because she's seein' somebody else on the side?"

"No, not because of her, but because of *you*. Because of all the people *you* see on the side. You are always over here with your friends, or looking in the mirror with yourself. You are never with her. It just looked to me like you don't care."

"Well, then don't look. It ain't none of your business," El É answered. The unexpected criticism had caught him off-guard and made him forget to react with hostility. The homeys were all too ready to remind him, though. Jinete spoke up. Sometimes lately, he just wasn't feeling El É. First the bullshit drama about stealing and now these signs of weakness. This was crap. He was supposed to be representing!

"Hey, man, don't you see? He's tryin' to make it his business. You got yourself a rival, El È!" he fairly shouted.

Everyone waited to see some fireworks. But then, when El É screwed up his face at the absurdity of the mismatched rivalry, they all laughed. This kid was really kind of a joke, not even worth the sweat.

"I'm not trying to be a rival," Tzoquito said, oblivious to the danger he was running. "Sometimes I hear people's words and I see what they do and I still don't know what they're thinking. I'm sorry."

El É spoke grandly. "Well, I don't want to have to hurt you, Tzoquito. You're my brother, *¡puro Azteca!* We got to stick together. But you got to look someplace else for the females."

Brolo checked in on the fun. "Now how's he gonna get any females, lookin' all ratty like that? Yo, Tzoquito, man, ain't you got some decent clothes to put on your skinny ass?" Then he made a showy grab for Tzoquito's behind. Tzoquito jumped away and the others laughed.

"No! I just have these clothes and two more shirts that Don José gave me."

"Now, that's pathetic," Pinto said. "We've got to help this homey. Tzoquito, we're gonna hook you up. You need some new feathers, Indian. You got any money?"

"Money?"

"Yes! Money! *¡Lana, chico!"* Pinto shouted. Then he took out his wallet and flashed banknotes in Tzoquito's face. "See?" he squeaked.

"Money! Why?"

"Cause they don't take colored beads at the clothing store!"

"No, I don't have any...." Tzoquito had seen the stuff before, but was somewhat hazy on its value and its use. Pinto shrugged and turned away, just about to give up.

"... but Don José has some money in a box under the fancy bed."

Pinto laughed and spun back around and pointed at the Indian. "Well, now you're talking!"

5

It was dusk and the town had quieted down considerably. The marketplace near the main square, where the people from the far-flung hamlets or *parajes* of this municipality came to sell their produce and handicrafts, had been packed up and closed and all its vendors and buyers had dispersed. The ice cream popsicle man had wheeled his cart full of *paletas* back into its shed for the night. The boys who spent their afternoons kicking a soccer ball in the schoolyard near Lupe's house had all been called home to chores and meals and homework. And now there was no one about. El È only became aware of this quiet when he hesitated. When he stood there with his clenched fist ready to knock. It was hard to do and it felt like the whole town had stopped doing whatever it was doing, just to watch. Damn, it seemed that he had so many hard things to do all of a sudden. It would all be worth it, he told himself and he knocked on the door at the Melendez home. Almost immediately, Lupe came out.

He smiled weakly. "Wow, you're as fast as that little Indian. I just barely knocked."

"I was watching from behind the curtain."

"Were you waiting for someone?" He said with the first hint of suspicion.

"No, but when my housework is done, I just have nothing to do. You said so yourself, didn't you? There's nothing to do around here, besides watching life walk by in the street."

"I wish you wouldn't remember all the bad things I say. I would like you to remember the good stuff."

"The good stuff? Like what?" she said. Now this was a new gimmick, she thought.

"I don't know. I guess maybe we could think of something and then I can say it. The thing is, I want to start treating you right. Like my fiancée. Like the woman I will marry someday."

She sighed and looked away. "I don't get it, El È. You don't know me anymore than I know you. We are completely different. Why would you want to marry me? Why don't you go back to all your girls in L.A.?"

"Well, apart from the fact that I can't go back, I'm not even sure that I want to go back there." He hesitated a moment and then continued, part calculation and part sincerity, "Or that I even have anybody to go back to."

"That's a switch," she said. "Your first morning here you were talking like that was the greatest place on earth."

"I'll be honest, Lupe, there's a part of me that says no way to all this, I ain't gonna let my grandfather find a wife for me down the road in this *pinche colonia.*"

She crossed her arms impatiently, so he hurried to continue his thought. "But on the other hand, I feel so good now that I am here. I envy the people here. I envy you Lupe: your honesty, the way you know exactly what you need to do in your life. I don't have any of that in L.A. I know I will never have that clarity, but I want it for my children. I don't want them growing up on the streets, acting like fools and fakes. I want them to be real people from a real place."

Lupe had every intention to still be angry, but now she couldn't help but be impressed with this candor. "And you think that will happen for them here? This is no paradise, either."

"I know that, but with the help of a woman like you, yes, I believe these things can happen."

"But what will they live on here? What would we live on here? There is nothing around here to keep people going, except some little coffee and potato cooperatives. That's why your father took you across the border. And apparently, he does pretty well over there. So, what's going to stop you from wanting to go back there? I am afraid of that. It's not bad enough that that's another country, but all of you *emigrantes* act so rudely, so bad. I don't want to be a part of that and I don't want my children to grow up into that."

"That's what I'm saying. Believe me Lupe, I don't want that either. You know how to call it. There is nothing I want more in the whole world than to build a life for you and me and a family right here in Cielitos. And we can do it. I don't have much money right now, but I promise you, Lupe, very soon and I mean very soon, I'm going to have a whole lot more. Enough to invest in a little business. We could sell things like sneakers and cds and videos. There's a whole lot of stuff people don't know that they miss down here."

His words were like cold water in her face. Now the truth was coming back. He couldn't keep it hidden for very long. He was still the gangsta she had seen that first day. "What do you mean you are going to have a whole lot of money?"

"Just what I said. Me and my boyz are working on something..."

"Something? That deal you were talking about?"

"Yes."

"You think that makes me feel good, that you are going to invest some filthy drug money here for us to live on? To buy food for your children?"

"Who said anything about drugs? You take me for some big thug. I know we just met again this week after such a long time, but why don't you just try to believe me, why don't you open up your eyes?"

"Well, then what kind of a deal are you talking about?"

But now that he was encouraging her interest, he wasn't so sure that he wanted to tell. "Selling something," he said cryptically.

"Selling what?" Now she was getting impatient again.

"I can't tell you that."

"Why not?"

"I just can't tell you, Lupe. You just have to trust me."

73

"How can I trust you, Egilberto? You got thrown out of the United States when you got arrested for something or other, don't think I don't know. Then, you come down here with those *desgraciados*. You're talking about deals and money. I'm sorry, I don't trust you, that's all there is to it. And I can't promise myself to a man I don't trust."

"Lupe, a man doesn't have to explain himself every minute to his woman. That's what it means to be engaged to a real man, to be a macho."

"You're wrong about that, Egilberto."

"No, I'm not. There isn't a man in Mexico that has to beg his wife to believe him every time he goes out to earn his peso. That's life, that's the birds and the bees. If you don't like it, then maybe you should marry that sissy Indian and lead him around by the nose all you want."

"If that's what I want, that's what I'll do!" She said it without thinking and then when she did think about it, she wasn't embarrassed one bit.

"Good! But trust me, when you're kicking him out of bed at the crack of dawn to go to work at Burger King, you'll be begging me to jump in your bed to give you what you need."

"*¡Maleducado!* How dare you say that, Egilberto!"

"Good night!" he said, pointedly polite, as he was a bit insulted by the *"maleducado"* remark. He may have been a player, but he knew how to be a gentleman, sort of. El È turned his cap around forward and pulled the visor down over his eyes and he turned and strode away. Lupe watched and finally rushed back into the house and slammed the door.

****

Outside of town, the sun comes up earlier. And out there work starts even earlier than that. By ten o'clock in the morning, a whole series of tasks had to be accomplished before the onslaught of the midday heat. Don José entered the house. It was midmorning and he had already put in several hours of work, tending to the pigs and the cow, inspecting the little patch of corn. He flopped down on a chair. Abuelita was grinding corn for *masa* and cutting vegetables at her kitchen counter. Judging from all the arrayed ingredients, she was making something special. "Oh, just *flor de calabaza* soup and some other things," she said. Zucchini flower soup was one of Tzoquito's favorites.

"What a morning!" Don José said morosely.

"What about it?" she said, somewhat amused by his crankiness. "It's just the same as any morning," she didn't look up from her kitchen work.

"Just hotter. The sun is hotter than the face of an angry demon." He looked up when his idle complaint got no more reaction. "And too much work for one old man by himself. Now just when I got Tzoquito to where he can tell the difference between a hammer and a nail, he has started hanging around with those young people in town."

Abuelita gave a little laugh. "Ay, won't we ever learn, José? It is always the same. It is nature. When they learn to fly, it always comes as a surprise."

Don José thought about her words. She was right, of course. It always happened this way. They all left as suddenly as they came. He looked around at the old cabin, the place that had turned wondrous, turned magical with the arrival of Tzoquito. Now it was looking shabby and old all over again. And indeed it was old, all except for the weavings and yarn paintings that Abuelita had collected over the years, the work of her relatives and friends. They hung decoratively from the roof beams and on the walls and covered the embroidered, satin bedspread on the fancy bed. This monstrous piece of useless furniture had been a gift of their son, ostensibly to give the old couple a modern place to rest their bones at night, but Don José suspected that it was really meant as a sleeping place for their son's own spoiled children to use when they came here to visit. In any case, the elderly couple didn't mind. They accepted the frilly fetish installed in their farmhouse, an object which, except for its enormous dimensions, was like one of those dolls in elaborate fancy skirts set on a high shelf where no little girl might touch it. And the old couple continued to sleep where they always had, in hammocks strung from posts in the middle of the room.

Now Don José's glance fell on that fancy bed and he noticed something odd about it.

"What happened to the bed?" he asked.

"What about the bed?

"The spread is all rumpled and bunched. Were you resting on it this morning? You don't feel well?"

Abuelita stopped chopping and looked over at the bed. "I feel fine. I just came back inside just now from the vegetable garden."

"It looks like somebody has been sleeping there," he continued.

"No. Maybe Tzoquito. He was looking for you about an hour ago. He came into the house and left a little while later."

Don José shook his head, "Tzoquito wouldn't sleep on that thing anymore than we would. And besides, he didn't even sleep here at all last night," he added regretfully. But his eyes were drawn back to that bed. There was something about it that made him uncomfortable. He walked over to it and peeled away the covers that had recently been upturned. Just as he had feared, he saw that some things have been pulled out from under the bed. He bent down and looked. Among the tossed up objects was the wooden box. He picked it up slowly, reluctantly and he opened the lid.

It was empty.

"Ayyyy! Tzoquito! The cooperative's money! Tzoquito!" he wailed. Abuelita dropped what she was doing and came over to look.

"¡Ay, Dios mio!" she exclaimed.

"Who made him do it, Abuelita? Who made our Tzoquito steal this money?"

That same midmorning sun beat down on Cielitos, pushing the houses even further down into the dust, the dust that was everywhere: flying, settling and whirling about. Whirling in the tailwind of that great boat of a Chevy as it raced with a roar right out of town on the International Highway. It put the town quickly behind it and rode the highway, *la carretera,* downhill as smoothly as a river canoe on a mountain stream, descending through *Bochil* and further down into the lowlands.

Jinete had convinced El É to let them borrow the car to escape from Cielitos for a few hours and that had put them all in a celebratory mood. Music thumped so loud that the telegraph poles tingled as the Chevy passed. Nobody noticed, except Tzoquito, of course, who noticed everything. This was his first ride in a car and he was enjoying it tremendously. It didn't matter one bit where they were going and he had no clue, even when they passed a sign that said, *Pan American Highway* and another one that said, "Tuxtla Gutiérrez 30km," and even after Brolo shouted "Walmart! Woo-hoo!" These were all concepts that meant nothing to him.

They had spent the whole ride rapping along with the CD. Tzoquito joined in with them, rapping the words in English, almost as well as them. The fact was that his magic and binquizac thirst made words enter his body like liquid. He drank in the English that the homeys were speaking, just as he had been drinking in Spanish during the past few weeks. Whereas other people may take months to learn the most basic things about a foreign language, all human language was so delicious, so healing, so redemptive and so welcome to Tzoquito, that he could do the same learning in just a matter of days. By the time the car entered the parking lot of a modern shopping center, he was rapping in perfect unison with the others, mimicking every sound, as if he knew exactly what he was saying.

The car screeched into a painted spot and stopped. Jinete, Pinto, Brolo and finally Tzoquito jumped out and took a cool look around at the shopping plaza. The whole area with its bright colorful signs taller than any tree and its enormous buildings was wildly impressive to Tzoquito. To him alone – it seemed to leave the rest of the company cold.

"Pffft," Jinete said. "Come on, let's see if they sell anything in this big taco tent!"

There were sales bins right inside the front door. Tzoquito picked out a football jersey, size small, but Brolo pulled it out of his hand with a laugh. He brought him over to another bin and found the same one, only this one was marked XXXL.

"That means extra extra extra cool!" Brolo told him.

In the shoe department, Tzoquito inspected a sneaker with shiny metal studs above the toes. He liked that because they looked like claws. He liked it even more when Pinto showed him that when he pressed the heel, tiny lights ran around the perimeter of the sole.

Tzoquito stood in front of the mirror in the mens sportswear department. The mirror seemed very complicated, with unfolding parts and overhead lights. He barely knew where to look, because as soon as he looked in one section, he would notice out of one eye that his image was moving in another. But in any case, he was fascinated by the mirror with its plural images of him as a perfect, breathing human being.

While he stood there admiring himself, ever turning to catch his fleeting side image, like a dog chasing its tail, Brolo was looking through the jeans, pushing them along the racks looking for the gaudiest ones he could find. He held up a pair judgmentally. "What do you think about these, with the fuzzy pockets?" he said to Pinto.

"Hey!" Jinete's voice came from across the store. Brolo quickly dropped the acid-washed jeans and the three of them hurried back over to Jinete. It was obvious who was the boss in El É's absence.

"I found the barber!" Jinete called and he pulled Tzoquito along to a row of glassed in shops near the check out counters. In one of them, an elderly man with a sour expression stood with a sharp metal weapon in his hand. To Tzoquito's horror he was pulled along precisely to him.

Tzoquito watched sadly as the clumps of black hair tumbled down around him. He had only had this fine, delicate human hair for a few weeks and here it was disappearing. He sat bundled up in the barber's chair, feeling the mean little buzz of the metallic mouse that the brooding, silent barber passed hungrily all over his scalp. And in little time, his head was entirely shaved.

He didn't really like the way it looked, but there were always going to be things he didn't like at first, things that he would then grow into. The lack of hair would have to be one of them. And indeed, by the time they were walking back to the car with their packages, through the oily smelling blacktop parking lot, he liked the coolness of the air on his skin and the beating of the rays of the sun on his scalp.

"Feels good, right?" Brolo asked.

"Yeah."

"But now you gotta learn how to walk right," Brolo continued.

"I know how to walk!" Tzoquito said. "I've been practicing for weeks!"

Pinto laughed. "Yeah, but not practicing right!" With that, Pinto showed him an exaggerated limp, one that would look ridiculous outside of the most foolish teenage gathering.

"You gotta *limp!"* he said and the others laughed.

Tzoquito laughed too and immediately started imitating. It really wasn't that difficult for someone who had spent his entire life studying the every movement of a human being.

"That's it! That's it! You got it man!"

And the four of them cool limped all the way back to the car.

The curving street in front of the Melendez house was wide and bright in the twilight of sunset. The sidewalk there was very narrow, though and no good for a real promenade. But the roadway was much better. It was wide enough for a walker to make an impression from a good distance and it was paved with smooth, richly colored cobblestones. Tzoquito would have liked to walk these stones in his bare feet, with the satisfying slap of his fleshy soles against the stones, feeling the syncopated beat of their uneven surfaces under the rhythm of his cool gait. But this new sensation, gliding along on the soft, warm cushion of his blinking sneakers, was equally as good. Tzoquito was putting those sneakers to good use, as he walked back and forth in front of Lupe's house, practicing his limp.

After the third turnaround, Lupe came out of her house and stood there with her arms folded in front of her.

"Tzoquito! What are you doing?"

Tzoquito stopped and smiled. This walk seemed to have a magic attraction. "What do you mean? I was just walking by!"

Lupe stared at the football jersey that came down almost to his knees, the baggy khakis and the sneakers that peeked out from underneath them, with green running lights that moved in endless circles around the sole.

"Where did you get those clothes? You look like one of those thugs."

"You mean your fiancé. I wanted to buy some new clothes, so I went to the store."

"With what money?"

Tzoquito went silent and looked away. What should he tell her? He had an inkling from the homeys' howling and hooting that he had done something bad.

Miguel and Juanita came out of the house and ran up to Tzoquito with festive air.

"¡Hola, Tzoquito!" they shouted.

Tzoquito smiled broadly. *"¡Hola, niños!"*

Miguel stared in wonder at the brightly lighting shoes. "You look cool like that, Tzoquito!"

"Thank you, Miguelito," Tzoquito said as he ruffled the little boy's hair, the hair that reminded him for the tiniest moment of things that had been lost.

"Go inside, *niños*, Tzoquito and I have to talk now," Lupe said as she gave them a gentle shove back toward the house.

Miguel turned to his older sister. "Lupe, buy me some clothes like that! *¡Por favor!"*

"No, Miguel, we don't have money for such things! Go inside! Go!"

And as the children walked away, Lupe turned back to Tzoquito with a worried look. "But *you* have the money, Tzoquito. What money, Tzoquito? You didn't take the money from under Don José's bed, did you?"

Tzoquito suddenly felt a tinge of regret. "Why would you think that?"

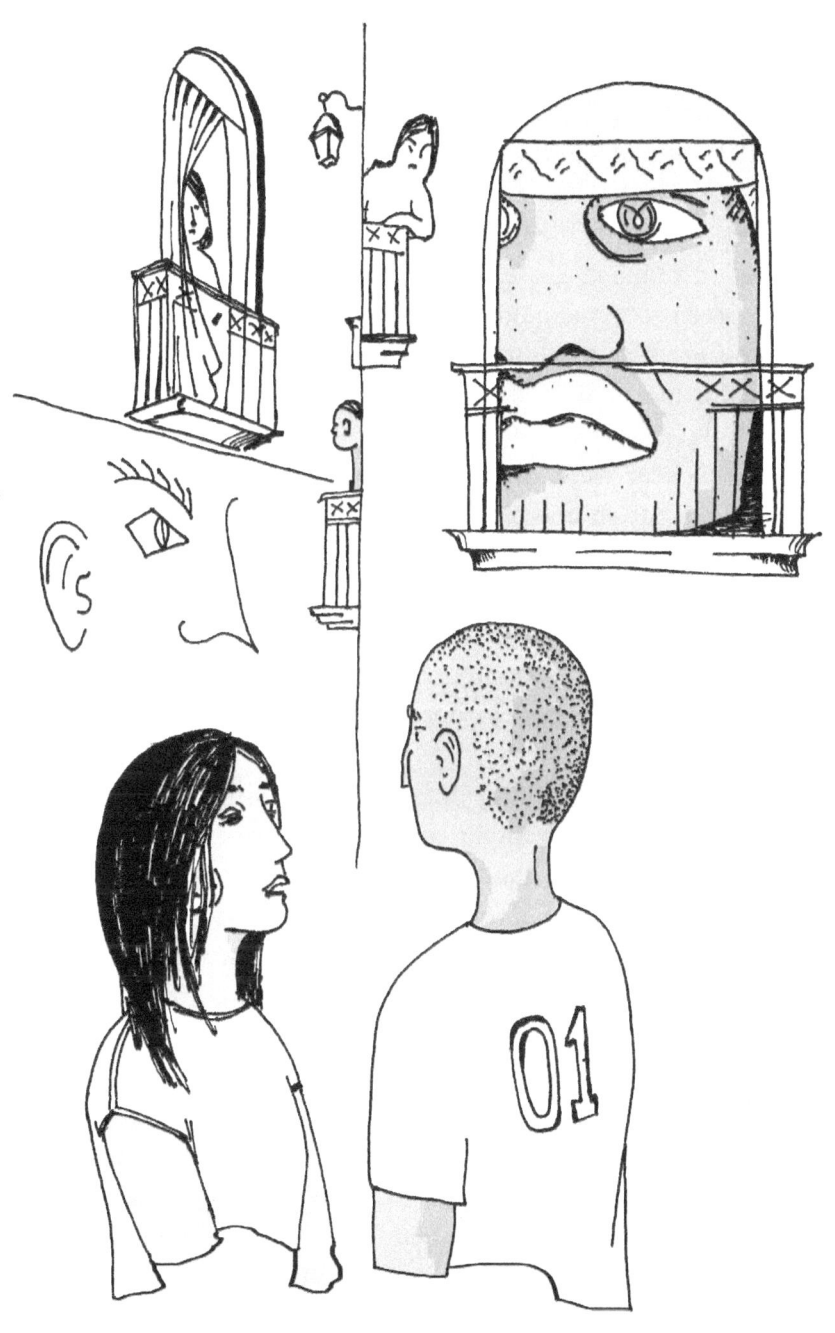

"Because it's missing, Tzoquito. And Don Jose thinks that you took it." She looked at him curiously. "And now all of a sudden you have these clothes? Did you take that money, Tzoquito? That money belongs to the farming cooperative. Without that money they can't pay their bills. It's a disaster."

"Really?"

"Yes! Tzoquito, please tell me that you didn't take the money."

"I didn't take it, Lupe," he answered immediately. Ah, sometimes it was so easy to make humans happy!

"You are sure you didn't take it? Abuelita says you went into the house this morning."

Still there was so much to learn. Apparently, just saying what she wanted to hear was not enough. So he spun out a bit more, hoping this would put an end to it. "I was looking for Don José. When he wasn't there, I left." Then he was relieved to see how this answer calmed her.

"Mentiras," one neighbor said dryly, her head bobbing with the word "lies" as she leaned on her railing just a few feet above their heads, her chin cupped in her hand. She looked away when Lupe glared up at her.

"There will be nothing but trouble as long as those boys from California are here," another lady said.

A woman across the way nodded her agreement and stage-whispered back, *"Son diablitos."*

"And now they are teaching this one their ways," the first woman jerked her head toward Tzoquito. *"¡Qué vergüenza!* Soon we'll have a whole gang of them right here in Cielitos!"

The neighbors were ostensibly talking to each other, but they made quite sure that their words were loud enough for the naive Lupe to hear. Resisting the urge to snap at them, Lupe took Tzoquito by the hand and lead him over to the alley at the side of her house, where her father had built a garden between the buildings. There, behind its wall, they would be out of view from the neighbors. But unfortunately not out of earshot, so she spoke low, so as not to be overheard anymore.

"Tzoquito, I don't want to tell you what to do, but I don't think you should hang around with those *cholos.*"

"Don't worry about me, Lupe. I learn very quickly."

"I'm just afraid that you're going to learn all the wrong things."

He spoke low too. He liked this game of voice changing. And he liked the way she had brought him to this shady corner. "I'll learn everything! The wrong things and the right things, too. When I came here to Cielitos, I didn't know why I came but now I have learned." Tzoquito took hold of her arms tenderly. "I came here to meet you."

She was exhausted. Tired of her predicament and tired of this whole town. She let him touch her arms, mostly out of sadness and fear that nothing would ever turn out the way it should. Then Tzoquito came closer still and kissed Lupe tenderly on the lips. She moved back.

"You shouldn't do that," she said.

"I didn't take the money, Lupe," he said, figuring it couldn't hurt to repeat it.

"No, that's not what I mean."

He let go of her. "I don't know why Don José thinks I took it. What do you think he'll do to me?"

"I don't know, Tzoquito."

"Please believe me, Lupe. I didn't take it!" Tzoquito had raised his voice. Lights went on in another neighbor's window.

"*¡Mentiras!*" She could hear that neighbor's voice come back again, faintly around the corner of the house. Lupe had believed him, but now this behavior, – now she wasn't so sure. Could Tzoquito be a liar, too?

She realized in spite of herself: the neighbors were right.

"You took it, didn't you!"

Too late, he realized that at a certain point, you have to stop insisting. So many unspoken rules! "No, Lupe, I swear!"

"And now you are lying, too!"

He didn't answer.

"Lying to me!"

Tzoquito covered his face with his hands.

"I can't believe it, Tzoquito! How could you let them convince you to steal that money?"

"I'm sorry, Lupe. I was stupid, I didn't even know what money was. I didn't even know it was important."

Truly, he was the strangest boy she had ever met.

"Oh, Tzoquito, what will we do now? Do you have any of it left?"

"No, nothing. But don't worry, Lupe, I will pay the money back!"

"How are you going to do that?"

"The homeys told me about some business they are planning. They said if I come along, they will give me some of the money."

"Are you crazy, Tzoquito? Do you know what they are planning?"

"No."

Lupe realized that they were talking loud again, so she lowered her voice.

"Of course not. You can't go with them, Tzoquito. They are planning a drug deal."

"*¿Cómo?*" In reality, he had no idea what she meant and it was useless for her to repeat it.

But she did so anyway and this time a little louder. "A drug deal!"

"*¿Cómo?*" Tzoquito repeated, still not understanding.

"*¿Cómo?*" said the neighbors in unison, just now understanding.

In frustration, Lupe shouted. "A drug deal, Tzoquito!" And she looked up, realizing that she had now said it loud enough for everyone to hear.

Now embarrassed, she went quickly back into her house and locked the door.

And then the neighbors took over.

"*¿Oíste? ¡Las drogas!*"

"What a plague that comes back to us from *el Norte*! Are the dollars really worth all this trouble?"

Now a third neighbor chimed in. "Someone should tell the police! And get them out of here once and for all!"

Tzoquito heard the neighbors and their words jumbled into his head but his thoughts were elsewhere, with Lupe inside her room.

"Lupe! Don't be mad," he called out consolingly. "Don't worry, did you hear that? Somebody will call the police and that will solve everything! I'm going to get the money and I'll give it back to Don José so he won't be mad anymore. Please don't be mad, Lupe! Lupe!"

But there was no answer, just the odd clucking from the balconies all around him. And Tzoquito walked away slowly into the darkened street, his unthinking sneakers blinking as happily as ever, as he exited the scene.

****

"Jinete!"

Much later that night, Tzoquito rattled the bars of the gate that lead into another yard in the neighborhood. That of Jinete's aunt. The gate was locked. He looked in to see what was there, under the moonlight. The presence of the homeys was evident everywhere. Plants in crooked and cracked pots had been dragged carelessly into the corner along with two broken chairs. There were empty bottles in cases piled up right in the path, as though waiting to be picked up or possibly left abandoned after a poorly executed chore. Nearby were a couple of bags of garbage and mounds of baggage and clothing belonging to the visitors from the North.

"Jinete! Jinete! Open up!"

Tzoquito could have easily jump right over the wall, as he had already done once before, but he didn't dare. Jinete was not the type of person he was going to fool around with. So he rattled the gate some more. Finally Jinete came running out of the house, wrapped in the blanket from his bed, against the midnight chill.

"Hey, what's the matter with you, man? You'll wake up my whole family!"

"It's me, Tzoquito!"

"Yeah, I know, I know. Who else would it be?" Jinete came up to the gate but made no motion to open it.

"Let me in! I've been walking around for hours. I'm tired but I don't want to go back home."

"Ha, ha. Afraid Don José found out about the money?"

"He did find out. Why didn't you tell me it was a bad thing to do?"

"I'm not your mamma, Tzoquito."

"Let me come with you tomorrow and help you with your business. Then maybe you can give me some money to pay back Don José."

"Are you crazy?"

"Please, Jinete! Let me come and make some money too!"

"What makes you think we need you hanging around, messing things up?"

"Brolo said I could come if you said it was okay."

"That's because he knew I would never say it was okay. And anyway, we're not sharing any money with you unless you earn it."

"Oh, I will earn it, Jinete. I don't know how yet, but you can be sure I will find a way. I know how to do lots of things."

"Well, you sure can run fast. That could come in handy. But no, man, forget it. You will fuck everything up."

"Please, Jinete, please! Otherwise I can never face Don José again! Please!"

"¡Cállate, *güey*!"

Finally Jinete took pity on the guy, or maybe just gave in to shut him up. He opened the gate and let him in. "You sleep out here in the yard. I'm going back to bed!" Jinete indicated a long car seat from the Chevy. "Here, sleep on Brolo's car seat. With his ass hangin' out of his pants, it took him no time to find one of his fellow perverts to shack up with in town. And Pinto's in a hammock in back."

Then Jinete disappeared back in the house without another word. Tzoquito tested the car seat but found it lumpy and pointless. Why fold yourself into this contraption when there were comfortable spots all around? He crawled around a bit on all fours and found a spot he liked on top of a bed of flowers. There he curled up and with a little whimper of self-pity and homesickness, he began to munch on some flower petals. Then, somewhat reassured, he closed his eyes for a good night's rest.

6

———•———

Early the next morning El É was back behind the wheel of the big Chevy. He drove up to Jinete's house and honked the horn. It seemed that now they really *were* cloning, when four homeys instead of the expected three, came bounding out of Jinete's yard: Jinete, Pinto, Brolo and Tzoquito. Tzoquito was wearing a long XXXL tee shirt with a cartoon bad boy on the front and the words *"Vato número Uno"* (number one bad boy). El É hadn't seen the transformation until now and he stared in disbelief.

Brolo shouted happily. "Hey, El É! We got a new recruit!"

EL É was in no mood for the joke. "You guys are nuts! There's no way we're taking the Indian with us."

"Hey, chill out, man," Pinto countered. "Look at him, man, all pimped out and ready to go! *Bien cholando!*"

Brolo laughed at Pinto's good cheer, as he and Pinto installed the back seat in the car. But the cheer failed to reach El É, who only frowned and glared.

"No fuckin' way!" came the response of their leader. Then he turned his fiery eyes to Tzoquito. *"Vete a la fregada!"* he said, Get out of here!

Tzoquito froze to his spot, unsure how to obey. When the seat was in place, the lieutenant and three foot soldiers stood back, staring in at El É in the driver's seat, waiting for somebody to say something. Jinete knew he would have to pull this together, so he got in the front seat, shut the door and spoke to El É, negotiation style.

"I'm with you, bro," Jinete said confidentially, "but these *payasos* think it's a good idea. If he does come, he's gonna work for his share."

"His share? You think we're splitting this one more way?"

"Think about it, man, that'll be a lot easier than you think. Look at him, *¡ese pendejo!* It's like he just discovered money yesterday. What's the difference between a one dollar bill and a one hundred dollar bill, besides a couple of zeros? Sure as hell *he* don't know."

El É stared straight ahead in anger, "You guys never know when to stop." Then with a barely perceptible nod, he finally gave his consent.

"Come on, get in, *soldados,*" Jinete called out to the others. "We got business today!" He looked back at the house nervously. "Hurry up, I don't want to be here when my aunt sees what Tzoquito did to her favorite flowers last night."

The footsoldiers all began jumping in gleefully.

"Business!" El É grumbled in exasperation. "Ha, you jokers think that people do business like this? You will never be anything but a bunch of wannabe gangstas no matter what you try!"

But the others were too excited to let El É spoil the party. Brolo got into the backseat, then Pinto laughingly pushed in the grinning Tzoquito, to sit between himself and Brolo. El É turned and glared at Tzoquito.

"You look ridiculous," EL É said, but Tzoquito's festive grin was undiminished.

"Thank you!" the Indian said in English.

With a great lurch, El É took the Chevy on the road and right out of town. They got on the state highway but did not descend toward Bochil. Instead they went another way, cruising along to ever higher elevations, as though rushing up to meet the sun as it climbed ever hotter in the sky on its levantine thrust. Jinete, like a real lieutenant, was sitting next to El É and their heads were like the two parents on a family outing: as long as the people in the back seat could see the back of their heads, everything was cool. You could do anything you wanted, just as long as you didn't make them turn around.

But Pinto had to risk it after a few stultifying miles of boredom. The festive mood had evaporated and no wonder: it was getting damn hot in there! He called out to the front seat.

"Yo, Jinete, move your head, man. You're in my breeze!"

"Move your own head, *güey,"* came the predictable answer.

"What does it matter anyway, these *pinche montañas* stink anyway," Pinto mumbled his sour grapes.

Now El É called out above the noise of the ride. "Yeah, what is that smell? It smells like birdshit or something."

"It's like cowfarts and chicken breath," Brolo said.

But Tzoquito knew better. "No, there's a small lagoon just on the other side of that hill. You smell frogs and fireflies, wild epazote and chicken herbs. And one tecuaht snake right over there." He pointed to the grasslands to his right.

Pinto stared at him, then said to El É, "I told you this homey's got talent."

"Yeah, except too bad we don't need a *pinche* bloodhound, *güey.*"

"I know how to smell!" Tzoquito bragged, using English for the second time. His seatmates looked at him in surprise.

"Hey, Tzoquito," Jinete asked. "Since when do you speak English?"

The others turned to look at Tzoquito, even El É eyed him in the rear view mirror. Tzoquito liked the way that looked – like two eyes floating up near the car ceiling, which sagged in billows just inches above their heads.

"Yesterday!" Tzoquito answered with a grin. "I learn fast!"

They drove for hours, stopping only to pee off the edge of the road and to buy sweet rolls and fresh coconuts to drink and scrape at roadside stands. It was a complicated route, with two or three turn-offs, each one onto a smaller road or a more treacherous slope up and down the cordillera of mountains welding the states of Chiapas and Tabasco together. At sunset, having finally descended to more moderate elevations, the big car turned off the paved road and after another ten or fifteen minutes of bumpy, dusty ride, it slowed down and pulled off the dirt track behind some bushes. In the distance, between the bush branches, there was a clear view of a farmhouse on a little hump of high land. Behind it was a chain link fence that extended all the way down into a hidden gulch. Beyond that fence they could make out the plastic covered mounds of an archeological excavation.

Everyone was silent for a minute, until Jinete spoke.

"Well, that's it, the caretaker's house at the entrance to the site."

"What do we do now?" Brolo said in a whisper, suddenly sounding concerned. There might be some hard work in being a gangsta.

Once again, El É had to take charge. "We gotta figure out a way to get into the cellar. Jinete, you're sure that's it? You're sure they've got the boxes in the cellar of that crumbling old house?"

"Yeah, man. My girl Araceli talked to her uncle just before we left L.A. He works there and he's got a big mouth.

He tells her whenever they find something good and when they pack it up to send to D.F."

"But what about guards, man?" Brolo said. "They probably got guards with guns and they probably shoot!"

"What guards?" Jinete laughed. "It's an old couple in there, must be a hundred and ten years old. They don't even know what the workers put in the cellar and they're too old to even go downstairs. All we gotta do is get them old people out of that house for a half an hour, we load up the car and get the hell out of here. And then it will probably be another two weeks before anybody even misses the stuff! By then we'll be long gone, payday done came and went!"

They thought for awhile. They were just now realizing that it was all easier said than done.

"But how?" Brolo continued annoyingly. "We don't even have one weapon between us!"

El É gave him an especially fierce look. "Our weapon is our wits!" he said, thumping his own head hard, till it hurt.

"Yeah," Pinto agreed. "Our withs!" He misunderstood, but that was OK – he liked this new expression. "We gotta flush them out," Pinto said with a gangsta flip of his arm.

"That's right," El É agreed. Pinto basked in the glow of this recognition. "Scare them out and get the boxes while they're gone."

"But what would scare them out?"

"I know!" Brolo said. "We'll tell them it's a bomb scare! They have to evacuate and we've got to take out all the suspicious packages!"

He looked around for high fives of approval but then got a reaction he hadn't expected. When the laughter died down, everyone got quiet again, to do some serious brainstorming.

"A binquizac!" Brolo shouted bright. "Yo, Tzoquito, go and scare them out, *güey*!"

Tzoquito nearly jumped at the mention of that word. It was the first time he had heard it from any of them. He hadn't realized that they even knew it. "A what?" he asked.

"A binquizac, hombre," Brolo continued. "Hey, man, don't you know? That's what they call you in Cielitos. They say you're a jungle man. Why you think everybody shuts their doors when you walk down the street, homey?"

Tzoquito thought about it. About all the doors that he had seen slam in that town, about all the backs of people scurrying away at his approach.

Jinete turned around and looked at the backseaters for the first time in this conversation, but for once it was not to berate them. "Hombre, that might really work! They're probably superstitious old fucks. You guys can get outside the windows late at night and scare the shit out of them and send them out into the woods. Then me and El É will drive up and we'll all go in like pirates and get the boxes!"

The night got dark. As was the custom in this deep country, nighttime meant sleep and in the stillness of the countryside, an old man and an old woman stepped wordlessly around in their farmhouse preparing to go to sleep. Odd jobs and mending put away, food wrapped in the cupboard, water and gas turned off at the source. They knew the sounds of their house by heart, a simple repeating repertoire of squeaking hinges, settling plaster and creaking wood and they listened to its soothing regularity as they folded their clothes. But when they heard a rustle outside of the house, they stopped what they were doing and listened together, trying to decipher the animal. Then a pebble hit the window – that was no animal. The man spoke to his wife in *Nahuatl*, the language of Central Mexico.

"Who could that be?"

But his wife answered with another question. "Who comes to the window and not to the door?"

Then they heard a cry: two voices in disunion. Pinto and Brolo were shouting outside. *"¡Eeeeiii! ¡Ustedes! ¡Húyense!"*

Their voices were shrill and ridiculous. They made the old couple immediately think of a teenage prank.

"¡Eeeeiii!" It came again.

It sounded like they had learned their craft as trick-or- treaters at some childish Halloween in L.A.

The old man called out weakly. He was old enough to know that often the most dangerous people in the world are its idiots.

"¡Ey! ¿Quién es?"

Brolo, Pinto and Tzoquito were crouching behind some bushes just outside the window. Pinto was already getting impatient. He shouted out in irritation, forgetting to put on the Halloween spooky voice and just using his own usual squeak. *"¿Qué te importa, cabrón? ¡Córrense de aquí!"*

The old woman opened the door and looked around. Her husband crowded in the doorway with her. He had a shotgun in his hands.

Unintimidated, the old woman called out, angrily. "What are you talking about, run away from here? We're the caretakers here, we're not going anywhere! Who is that?"

Silence. The three homeys looked at each other. Brolo shrugged his shoulders, at a loss what to say. They hadn't expected the old people to be so uncooperative.

Then Pinto got an idea. He started howling like a high school coyote. And when the other two joined in, it was a remarkable noise. One of them sounded especially convincing.

The old man took a step forward. "Come out and fight like a man! We're not afraid of you, we're not afraid to die, either. Who is it?"

Brolo's pride was wounded. After all, he had been good enough for a speaking role in "Cats" in high school. He shouted out in a deep, rough voice. *"¡Somos los binquizaques!"* We are binquizacs!

More silence. The old couple looked at each other. Then the woman whispered to her husband in Nahuatl. "What's a binquizac?"

The old man turned once again to the night air. "What do you want with us?"

Fully disgusted with their constant questions, Brolo answered again, forgetting his theater training, just shouting in his own voice. "We're enchanted dogs! Just leave! Get out of the house! Run away and don't look back and don't come back for two hours!"

Then another voice was heard. "What's going on?"

The three homeys peeked up from the bushes and saw that a young man had joined the old couple. He was wearing boxer shorts and sandals and a guard uniform shirt. He yawned and slapped a mosquito on his leg.

"Some crazies!" the old lady said to him furiously. They must be drunk. They say they are enchanted dogs." Now she turned back to the unseen intruders and shouted in a scratchy voice. "What do you take us for, a bunch of fools? You are no binquizac! What do you want here?"

Silence. What should they say? They hadn't planned on telling the old couple what they wanted to do there. And now there was this other guy, they hadn't prepared for that.

"Think quick, hombres!" Pinto whispered/squeaked. " That guy in his underwear is coming right toward us!"

Suddenly a horrible sound came from right among them. Tzoquito let out a wild laugh, like a monkey, a long rippling chain of inhuman giggles that sent vibrations of unbearable chills down the spines of his buddies. Then he followed this with a rattling sound that brought images of hybrid monsters of incalculable proportions.

The old couple were immediately taken aback in fear and the sleepy guard was finally shaken awake and stopped fast in his tracks.

But just for good measure, Tzoquito repeated it: the laughter, the evil giggle and the deadly rattle.

"*¡Los binquizaques!*" The old man repeated the word in the smallest whisper to his wife. "What do they want with us?"

"What do we want?" Tzoquito replied to that whisper in oldest Nahuatl, a language he spoke perfectly well. "Just what we said! Get out, *cabrones!* Go! Go! Go!"

His voice had an electrifying effect on the old couple. They looked around them to see who could have heard their tiniest whisper. "Don't look at me!" the guard said, just as terrified as them.

"Go! Go! Go!" it said. That electrifying voice, they could hear it coming from all directions at once. From one side and from the other.

"Do you hear that?" the old man said in wonder.

Tzoquito once again let out the laughter and the rattle. Pinto and Brolo held their ears and said "SSSSHHHHHHH!" and "EEEEEE!" attempting to drown out the piercing sound, but this only added to the general roar of it all, as Tzoquito threw their voices against the walls of the house and the hillsides along with his own.

"Come on!" the woman shouted. "Let's go! Just do what they say!" She was finally convinced.

And so were her husband and the guard, too. In a frenzy the man dropped his shotgun, useless against the forces of magic and the three of them started running across the field, toward the stream that ran in the bottom of the gulch on its way to the great river.

"Keep going!" Tzoquito shouted all around them. "And don't come back for two hours. Did you hear me"?

"Yes, yes, we heard you! We won't come back for three!" the old man assured them.

"Run, Pedro, run quickly! *¡Ay, que malasuerte!* They're going to eat all of my tortillas!" the woman wailed. The guard was already disappearing up ahead of them.

"And don't look back!" Tzoquito added, beginning to really enjoy this.

"Keep running, woman!" the old man said breathlessly. "Those demons must be right behind us!"

As fast as they were going, the old people moved pretty slowly. It took them a long time to disappear down the path, even with Tzoquito constantly whooping just to prod them along. When they had finally gotten a good distance, Tzoquito started laughing uncontrollably, satisfied with his newfound ability to harness the power to scare the daylights out of humans. Pinto and Brolo stared at him and slowly pulled their hands away from their ears.

"Wow, Tzoquito!" Pinto said. "You're a freakin' savage!"

"Yeah, but he sure got the job done!" the other chimed in. "That was tight, Tzoquito! We didn't even have to run after them. Come on, let's go look for the car!"

The three got up from the bushes, just as the big car pulled up, with its headlights off. El É and Jinete jumped out and all of them ran into the house. The homeys found their way into the cellar and in a few moments Brolo, Pinto and Tzoquito were coming out with cardboard boxes to load in the trunk. And they went in and out, in and out, until they got everything that had been hidden below the feet of the old couple. Eventually, Pinto came running out of the house with the last carton and dropped it on the ground, slumping down breathless on top of it. Jinete was leaning against the Chevy, as he had been doing for awhile now, supervising the action.

"That's it, ain't it! That was the last box. Now, pack that one in and let's get out of here," he said, as he chewed importantly on a tortilla.

Pinto picked up the box once more and took it the last few paces to the car. Brolo pushed him back though just as he arrived.

"No, man," Brolo said, shaking his head. "That last box ain't gonna fit in the trunk. You're gonna have to sit with it under your feet." He slammed the trunk shut for emphasis.

El É was already at the wheel and everyone else wanted to pile into the car at once and get out of there, so Pinto had no choice but to comply without complaint. But although he was by far the smallest of the bunch, or maybe precisely because of it, he had worked the hardest and now he was at the point of exhaustion. As the homeys jostled each other to get in, he staggered to keep that last box in his arms. He very quickly lost control of it and it started slipping around in his arms as though of its own impulse, like a big cardboard jumping bean. Jinete reached over and grabbed it just as it was about to crash to the ground.

"Go on, get in!" Jinete commanded scornfully to Pinto and the other two soldiers, as he stood there holding the box. When they were all three squeezed in back there, Jinete leaned in to dump the box on their laps. Best put it in the middle, he thought. He looked at Tzoquito in his usual spot in the middle and he spoke.

"Hey, Tzoquito!"

But Tzoquito didn't answer. He was nervously preoccupied with something else: sniffing around him, the air, his shirt, his neighbor's necks; like a dog checking for something very suspicious. Jinete finally shouted and handed him the box.

"Hey! *¡Patán!*" Jinete called out roughly, and a startled Tzoquito looked back at him. "Stop practicing your smelling and make yourself useful. Hold onto this!"

"Yo, Jinete, be cool, man," Brolo said. "Tzoquito did good tonight. You shoulda seen those little old people run for the hills when he started screamin'."

"Yeah, I heard it," Jinete answered. "Me and just about everybody else in the State of Tabasco – not the coolest strategy."

Tzoquito smiled at Brolo, appreciating the invitation to once again bask in his success, but his face immediately changed to one of concern as Jinete shoved the big box onto his lap. He looked down uncomfortably at the flaps that came up almost to his chin and he began sniffing at it with distaste. This was the bad smell right here and now it was sitting right in his lap.

Jinete jumped in and the car started moving forward with a jerk. They continued going in the same direction, since El É thought it would be bad luck to ever retrace their route. They made slow, circuitous progress, riding up into the mountains and then descending back down to the lands sloping toward Villahermosa. In fact, in no time they were lost and way off course, but it took them a couple of hours to figure that out and a couple more to find their way back to a road that could lead them in the right direction.

By now it was morning, with the sun peeking up at the end of a row of low hills, burning feverishly at the backs of their necks. And even though they had only had one short nap all night, they were animated. Jinete was bopping his head to the music only he could hear in his earphones. El É was driving energetically, looking around at mirrors and moving objects in all directions, scanning for anything that looked suspicious. Pinto and Brolo were practicing a rhythm, drumming time on the car doors.

Only Tzoquito was quiet and unmoving, looking down with a worried stare at the box in his lap, as though afraid to take his eyes off of it.

"What is in this box?" Tzoquito asked for about the fiftieth time.

"Nothing, man," Brolo answered, once again.

"No, Brolo. There's something in the box," Tzoquito protested.

"Yeah, I know there's something in the box, Tzoquito. That's why the box is in your lap! Forget it, man, it's not important."

"It doesn't smell good," Tzoquito whined.

"Big deal. Nothing smells good around here."

"No, I mean it. It smells bad, like bad luck."

"What are you talking about?" Pinto was starting to get irritated. "You country people are superstitious about everything! It's just some rocks. Forget it."

"Some rocks?" Tzoquito continued, finally getting some information. "I know about rocks."

He started to open the box. Pinto grabbed his hand. "Whoa, hold on, man. Don't open the box."

"Why not? It doesn't smell good."

Tzoquito went back to pulling on the flaps. Pinto stopped him again and raised his voice. "Don't open the fucking box, *güey*! These boxes are supposed to arrive signed, sealed and delivered!"

Tzoquito stopped and stared at him. Then he stared straight ahead and tried to forget about the box oozing bad luck right there on his lap.

THE BACKSEATERS

More time passed. A couple of hours later they were still riding along looking for the state highway, but now at least they knew where they were. Things had quieted down considerably, too. El É was no longer so conscientious about checking the mirrors or the passing objects: whatever was gonna happen was gonna happen. Brolo and Pinto were slumped asleep on either side of Tzoquito, their heads at odd angles to avoid the late morning sun that streamed violently through the windows with inexplicable vigor. Jinete had his eyes closed too and the only sound was the tinny thump from Jinete's earphones, but it was not clear whether he was still hearing it at all, given that his head had stopped bopping long ago.

Besides the driver, only Tzoquito was wide awake, sweating. It wasn't the sun, because the sun did not bother him at all, even though he could tell that the sun was in a foul mood this morning. He was sweating in fear and looking at the box in his lap. He couldn't resist any longer. He slowly began to open it, as quietly as possible, without waking the others. He got the flaps open and looked down at the contents.

It was a carved Olmec mask. An ancestor, but not just any ancestor, it was a smooth jade ancestor covered with precious stones and looking back at him from a few inches away. It was obviously a very important ancestor, with the notches of human sacrifice etched down the side of its face like tears. As Tzoquito stared at this fearsome being, the mask slowly began to move, slowly coming to life. The eyes of the mask widened and the edges curled in anger. The neutral facial features transformed into a grimace of fury and rage and the mouth opened to reveal sparkling bone teeth that were just now sharpening to points that could rip the flesh off a wild boar. Tzoquito was terrified. What had they done? Why had they kidnapped this dangerous ancestor? The stench was billowing up at him now, the air was fast becoming poisonous and he couldn't breathe. He began to hyperventilate.

Then a low sound started coming up out of his own throat, in spite of his desire to stay quiet. A whimper, a moan, a groan and finally a great, piercing wail.

"Ayyyyyyyyyyyyyyyy!" he wailed and his head bobbed up and he found himself staring at the roof of the Chevy .

"Owwwwwwwwww!" his lips rounded and he was howling like a crazed coyote from Hell.

Everyone came alive. El É swerved on the road at this awful sound and the other three jumped up in their seats. They all began talking at once, shouting to be heard over Tzoquito's infernal voice.

"Holy Shit!"

"Ow, man, my ears! OWW!"

"Shut up, man!"

"What the fuck!"

El É pulled over to the side of the road, unable to drive. Now Tzoquito was thrashing around in his seat, still howling at the top of his lungs, staring at the roof of the car, as though he could not lower his face.

"Get it out of here!" he finally managed to say. "Get this box out of here!"

"What are you talking about?" Pinto shouted. "Calm down, man!"

Tzoquito tried to push the box away from him, anywhere, preferably out the window. Pinto and Brolo managed to restrain him. Brolo got him into a head lock and put his hand over Tzoquito's mouth to stop the shouting but he quickly pulled it away when he realized that he was in danger of losing a couple of fingers.

"What's the matter with you, man?" Jinete asked.

Tzoquito took in a deep breath and tried to answer the lieutenant's question as rationally as possible. "In the box! There's an ancestor in the box! He's very angry. We shouldn't have taken him from his resting place. We have to bring him back."

Jinete put his hands up to his head and slumped back in his seat. "You're fuckin' nuts, man."

"I'm telling you! We've got to bring him back. He is angry and he is scared. He will take revenge on us. We have to return him to that cellar."

"No, Tzoquito," Jinete said forcefully.

"*¡Si! ¡¡Síiiiii!!*" Tzoquito countered.

102

"NO!" Jinete repeated. "Maybe we should put you back in that cellar, asshole, but we ain't gonna put that box back there. So shut the fuck up."

"Ayyyyyyyyyyyyyy! Owwwwwwwwwwwwwwww!" Tzoquito howled in response, his face back up, his neck straining on his shoulders, trying to get the slightest extra distance from that box.

"Shut the fuck up, man!" El É shouted, unheard under the terrible noise.

Tzoquito went back to struggling and howling and pushing the box as far from his face as possible. How could anybody breathe in this car with that stench? His two seatmates were kept busy trying to hold him down and to keep the box from flying out the window. El É turned to Jinete.

"What are we going to do with this lunatic? I can't drive with that shit going on. And what if some cop sees this? They'll be all over us. You gotta shut him up!"

Jinete was furious. "We should throw that *perrito* out right here!"

El É turned around to the backseat and the commotion there. "Hey, Tzoquito, shut up! Shut up before we throw you the fuck out of here!"

Pinto got his hands on the box and shoved it down behind his legs, out of sight. Gradually, Tzoquito began to calm down again. Brolo and Pinto relaxed their grip on him and Brolo, who had his jacket-wrapped arm over Tzoquito's mouth, took it away and replaced it with Tzoquito's hand, setting that firmly over Tzoquito's own mouth. Tzoquito went quiet. With peace restored, El É started the car and returned to the road. Maybe they would be able to get home after all.

But it didn't last long. Very soon Tzoquito was sniffing around himself once more and very quickly he discovered the box. His eyes widened: the box was now on the floor with Pinto's fat, smelly feet planted firmly on top to keep it shut. How would the mask react to that disrespect? He stared, fixated and he pointed with his free hand at Pinto's dirty sneakers, but when he tried to speak he could only whimper from behind the clasp of his other hand over his mouth. Inevitably, that whimper was once again rising from his throat and once again becoming louder and louder. His hand popped off his mouth, his head went back and he was howling, almost immediately as loud and as wildly as before.

"Ayyyyyyyyyyyyy! Owwwwwwwwwwwwww!"

El É pulled over once again. "Freak! I can't drive with that noise!"

Jinete turned around and started shouting. "Get out! Get the fuck out, Tzoquito!"

Pinto and Brolo restrained Tzoquito once again. "What the hell are we gonna do?" El É asked.

"Just throw him out!" Jinete shouted at his leader, getting tired of his indecision.

"No, we can't do that!" El É answered.

"Why not? Don't worry about your girlfriend! Just throw the motherfucker out!"

El É gave Jinete a hostile look. Brolo and Pinto redoubled their efforts to quiet down Tzoquito as it became clear that their new friend was seriously in danger of getting tossed.

"We just can't," El É said. "It's not about my girlfriend. We brought him here. It's just not right, we can't leave him in the middle of nowhere. And anyway, people will start asking him all kinds of questions and he will tell them everything and before you know it they will be all over our asses. We just gotta get him quiet."

"Get him drunk, that'll shut him up," Brolo suggested. "But where? Anywhere we go, he's gonna be howlin' and carryin' on like a wild animal."

El É turned around to Pinto, "Hey, man, let's go to your cousin Kweeche's house, the one you were telling me about. We can get there in a half hour from here."

"What? Kweeche?" Pinto spit out the name. "No, man, I hate that *cholo* fuck. And if he finds out what we have in the car, he'll have our asses. He thinks this is his territory!"

Jinete laughed with scorn. "His territory? That fool ain't got a pot to piss in, much less territory!"

"I know," Pinto said. "He's totally delusional. And a bipolar psycho, too. His parents sent him down here from L.A. to get rid of

JINETE

him because he wouldn't take his medicine. He thinks some druglord kingpin set him up to control the hills, but it was really just my uncle with the money from his tequila ice cream business."

"Control the hills!" Jinete repeated. "He can't even control his bladder if you stare at him hard enough."

"Still, he's nuts," Brolo said to back up Pinto. "You don't know him, El É. He's convinced that he's some kind of district chief or something. He got himself some thugs and some gun molls from central casting and the guns to go with it! He's gonna definitely see this as a move on his turf and he's gonna be mucho pissed!"

"Meanwhile, if the real thugs knew about him, they'd squash him like the fat little bug he is," Jinete said.

El É made up his mind. "Hey, we've got no choice, we gotta get off the road someplace. Someplace discreet!" he drew out this last word long, just to showcase his high rent vocabulary. "Nobody's gonna tell Kweeche what we have in the car, man," he said. "So everybody calm down. We'll just go up there and get this Indian wasted. From the looks of him, two shots of firewater should do the trick. That's all, just knock him out, then drive off, nice and cool."

"That's it, man," Jinete said taking control. "That's the thing to do, otherwise I'm gonna put that howling dog out on the side of the road myself."

El É may have resented Jinete's aggressive manner, coming after he had already stated their course, but he didn't show it. Without saying a word, he started the car and got moving again, as Tzoquito's howl started up again. He turned off the main road and started on the way to their new destination.

7

A half hour later, the car pulled up in front of another farmhouse. It had been visible from afar, but up close it was obscured by a stand of decorative palms and other leafy plants gone wild. When they turned into the driveway and the house suddenly came back into view, they saw that two unshaven men the size of WWF wrestlers were standing on the porch, checking out the arrival. As the Chevy drove up and stopped, they had braced themselves into a defensive wall and when the car doors opened, the two men seemed to pump themselves up a couple of sizes bigger. A third man was standing behind them, peering out. He was a little round man half concealed behind their bulk.

Pinto was the first to step out of the Chevy and as he stood up, the little round man on the porch pushed the beefy biceps out of his way and squeezed out as though from behind a curtain. He crossed his arms and did his best to imitate their wide-legged stance but ruined the effect with an irrepressible silly grin. He was Kweeche.

KWEECHE

"¡Pinto! ¡Hijo de puta!" Kweeche said, "son of a bitch" being a term of endearment he reserved for close family members. "What are you doin' around here?"

Though he seemed to be welcoming him, Kweeche didn't move one inch closer. He stayed put on the top step of the porch, perhaps afraid to step away from the security of his gorillas, or maybe just to maintain his height advantage. He was extremely short even compared to Pinto. Thus Pinto and everyone else, for that matter, would have to come to him.

Pinto started walking toward him. His body was still aching from the back seat tussle and he tried not to show it.

Jinete got out too and came around in front of the car windows to block their view of El É and the two clowns left inside. No use raising suspicions right from the first impression.

"Hey, cuz!" Pinto said with hardly scraped up cheer. "What's happening? Long time, no? sí? Ha ha!" He gave his cousin the most elaborate *raza* handshake he could muster, given the circumstances: fingers, hand, fist bump and thumbs.

Unfortunately, there was an undeniable rumbling emanating from back inside the car and Kweeche's men were already straining to look around Pinto and Jinete to see what was in the back seat.

What was in the back seat was Brolo and Tzoquito, who instead of getting out, were struggling between themselves. Brolo was shoving the box onto the floor and at the same time trying to protect it from Tzoquito's frantic kicking. Then, with that accomplished, they both busied themselves pulling at their shirts, trying to wipe the sweat from their faces. Brolo leaned over to El É just as the driver was opening the door to get out.

"Fuck!" Brolo whispered as he shook his hands around trying to cool them down. "That box was burning my hands! How'd it get so damn hot?"

"Just make sure you cover it with that jacket so these gangbangers don't see it."

El É, Brolo and Tzoquito got out, hiding the box hurriedly under Brolo's hoodie as they left the car.

You know my homeys from L.A., right?" Pinto nodded at the others, as they unfolded themselves to full height.

Kweeche snorted derisively at the sight of them. "Oooh, the famous El É!" he spit the words out sarcastically. "So, we finally meet! To what honor do we owe this..... honor." He got all tangled in his words but he quickly recovered. He turned back to Pinto and eyed him intensely. He put on an evil smile. "You brought your whole crew here! What are you, trying to mess with my territory?" he got right to the point, as a joke, of course. But a joke with a serious barb attached to it, filed down to a razor sharp point. Kweeche had seriously messed people up in the past, without a moment's notice. So much so, that the meds were not some quack doctor's advice; they were strictly court-ordered.

"No, man, we're just chillin' in Meh-Hee-Ko, that's all." Pinto tried to control his voice but it was getting higher as he spoke.

"When did you start makin' social calls? What's this all about, cousin?"

"Well, we got our boy, Tzoquito, here, ..."

He started unraveling the yarn that they had invented along the road. As he was telling it, he prayed that it would sound at least halfway plausible to the suspicious, dangerous cousin. "He's got himself in over his head, did some pills or something and he's been jumping around like a crazy *chango* monkey the past ten miles. We need to calm him down before we hit the highway."

And indeed, Tzoquito was in bad shape. He was disheveled and sweaty and could barely stand up straight. He looked like he was in danger of dropping down onto all fours and running away into the hills. Pinto pulled him up and over close to Kweeche. With the little *cholo* still on the top step of the porch, they were eye level. Kweeche went through a repertoire of three or four different mean glares and the two goons crowded Tzoquito in on both sides, with their own bullish looks. Tzoquito was still having trouble straightening up and now he looked from one to the other of the faces, two of them scary by profession and the other simply psycho. Indeed, they were a formidable sight, but compared to what he had just seen in the box, this was like looking into the faces of kittens. He managed a weak smile for Kweeche, nonetheless.

"Hola," he said.

Kweeche began laughing. "Where'd you get this little monkey? What're you, robbing the village cradles looking for playmates?"

"He's my neighbor in Cielitos," El É said, suddenly protective. Already he did not like this little Kweeche pig. "We just took him for a ride in my Chevy."

"Don't front wit' me, *pinche payasos,"* Kweeche said fiercely, the laughter gone. "You here cause you want to hole up till dark. So you can figure out a way past that police roadblock down near the highway." He pointed his finger at the cringing Pinto. "What have you got in the car? You movin' weed? This is my territory, cousin!"

"No, man, if we had something, would we be so stupid to come here right to your house?" Pinto asked. The other homeys look at each other uncomfortably.

Pinto continued. "For real, man, we just wanna have some beer wit' you and chill out, that's all. We been driving in circles for hours."

But El É's attention had been drawn by something else Kweeche had just said. "What roadblock?"

For all his fearsomeness, Kweeche was a gossip. Maybe it was from staying holed up in that farmhouse for months at a time, or maybe it was the meds. He explained. "It's been on the police radio all morning. They've been setting up roadblocks all over the area to inspect cars. Somebody broke into some archeological museum last night and stole a whole bunch of shit."

"Wow, last night, you say?" El É said pointedly sarcastic, as he looked over at Jinete. "I would think it would take them at least two weeks to figure out something was missing. I didn't realize that the cops were so efficient here. They must be right on those guys' tails."

"That's right! The Judicial Police. And the Highway Patrol. And the state police, the *federales* and the Finance Police!" Kweeche said enthusiastically. "You can ruin what you want in Mexico but don't fuck with *the* ruins. Especially if you haven't paid for the privilege."

There was uneasy silence but Kweeche didn't notice, as he continued to tell the news. "They're checking every suspicious car that comes through, inside and out. And there ain't nothing more suspicious than a car full of lame wannabe *cholos* like you." He checked out the reaction of his uninvited guests to his latest clever dig. But somehow, they seemed preoccupied with their own thoughts. One of his many sixth senses told him that he was onto something. He narrowed his eyes some more, until they looked like little black slits resting on top of his puffy brown cheeks. "So I wouldn't be standing face to face with the famous grave robber art thieves right now, would I?"

Pinto laughed unconvincingly and the other homeys followed suit. "Yo, Kweeche! What do we look like? Does it look like we're giving Mona Lisa a lift in this Chevrolet?" He waved back at the car but made no attempt to give Kweeche a clearer view.

Kweeche did not smile, however he was slightly amused. "Yeah, okay, what was I thinking, right? I musta been nuts!" Then he became fierce again and double-take quick, as he checked all their faces for any unwelcome agreement. His guests froze like kids playing statue. "But I know you're carryin' something. So if you want some help gettin' through, you better be ready to share some of the goodies with your cousin Kweeche."

Pinto bravely stood his ground. "Yo, back off, man. We're just here for a friendly visit, that's all. I ain't seen my cousin in years. Not since they put you away in the, in the..."

"In the clinic."

"Yeah, the clinic."

Kweeche relented, if only to stop his cousin from protesting in that girly voice of his. It was embarrassing. So he stepped back and nodded for them to enter the house.

"You're family, Pinto. I believe in family. Come on in. But if that kid came here to straighten out, he's in the wrong place, that's for damn sure. Nobody leaves Kweeche's house sober!"

Kweeche's two goons nodded and worked up a tooth baring smile that looked more like a threat. They scrutinized Tzoquito contemptuously as the group entered the house.

"And if he goes into cardiac arrest," Kweeche continued, "he's your corpse, not mine!" His own joke struck him as particularly funny and he laughed out loud.

The house was fairly large inside, with many rooms and to their dismay, full of strange people. Most of them ignored the newcomers and remained unintroduced, — Which was okay, since the elaborate handshaking was getting old very quickly. In one inner room there were two big thugs sitting around in a cloud of cigar smoke, under cheap wood paneling and a dogs-playing-poker tapestry. The thugs were playing poker. There was a shag rug on the steps leading upstairs where heavy footsteps and girlie laughter could be heard. Then, beyond the stairs there was a back porch where three local men were sitting around drinking beer. They wore wrinkled suits that bulged between the buttons and in odd places around their middles. It was quite a randomly assembled party. Apparently, such was the magnetic power of a very generous trust fund in the hands of a highly irrational trustee. In the kitchen two bleached blondes in tank tops and short shorts were making a mess, ostensibly cooking. One opened the refrigerator as the company entered and handed each newcomer a beer.

El É accepted the beer and a bowl of rice and beans and brought it all into the front room. He sat down next to a window where he could keep an eye on the car parked in the front yard. Kweeche and one of his men followed him with their eyes and noticed this, but were careful to make no sign of it, except to each other. Soon the whole party of newcomers was there in the front room, happily shoveling food into their mouths.

Kweeche turned his attention to Tzoquito. He watched with amusement as Tzoquito's bug eyes got ever larger while surveying all the various wonders of this house. When the boy wandered close, Kweeche reached out and upward and pushed the dazed Tzoquito down into an armchair. "Relax, baby boy. Now you're really in deep!" He laughed and lit a joint, just for the fun of it and when Brolo, Pinto and Jinete jockeyed to be first to get that fat reefer, Kweeche passed it to Tzoquito instead.

"Here, you hold onto this," he said to the puzzled Indian. "I'll set up these other guys with another one." Then he started another joint and set it in motion among the other three and walked away.

Jinete, Pinto and Brolo all stood close together, bopping to the beat of hip hop music on the stereo in an adjacent room, enjoying the smoke and their good luck getting their foot in this door and shutting Tzoquito up. This last one had even recovered his strength enough to get up and bop along with them. But the best of all, was when Kweeche and his men withdrew to another room to their own business, inviting El É to join them in their card game. That left the four of them blissfully alone.

"Hey Tzoquito, now you chillin', man," Brolo said after they had been there awhile. He, like the others, had had serious second thoughts about coming here, but now things were getting very cool.

"Yeah, this is cool," Tzoquito agreed, picking the word right out of Brolo's thought. "I can't believe all the cool things I have done in the past 24 hours."

Pinto started listing: "Got your fancy threads. Got your groove on, too, boy! Yeah!"

Jinete couldn't help but be sarcastic. "Robbed an old couple, sent them running for their lives...."

Tzoquito's grin suddenly dissolved into worry, but Pinto was right there to rescue it. "Ah, they'll be fine," he said. "They didn't even know what was down there in their basement and nobody's going to hold them responsible, with the guard standing right there."

"Yeah," Brolo backed him up, "as far as they know, we didn't touch anything except a few tortillas. And anyway, now they've got some good scary stories to tell their friends."

Tzoquito was back at ease. Perhaps too much at ease, considering how he chose to top off the list. "Yeah and best of all, I even kissed Lupe!"

Jinete stopped moving and stared at Tzoquito. "What?" Jinete demanded.

Once again unaware, Tzoquito explained from inside his smoky haze. "It was beautiful. Her lips were the softest things I've ever touched."

"Fuck, man!" Jinete said. He pushed Tzoquito with both hands. Tzoquito went spinning around, not even aware of the aggression. Pinto grabbed Jinete and pulled him away.

Brolo tried to placate. "Hey, Jinete, calm down, *güey*."

"That fucking *hijo de puta* is going too far. Now he's hitting on El É's girl."

"Hey, what's the big deal?" Pinto took up the thread. "Since when are you so worried about El É's girlfriend, anyway? She probably did it like girls kiss a little kid. They do shit like that all the time."

But Jinete was unconvinced. "I'm sick of everybody protecting that hick," he said, pointing at the still spinning Indian. "I'm sick of that punk messing everything up. It's time we got rid of him once and for all!"

The music suddenly got louder. They turned and saw that the door to the adjacent room had been opened. El É came stumbling out, holding his head. He groped his way toward the door.

"Hey, where you goin', man?" Brolo asked.

"I don't feel good. I'm gonna go sit in the car."

El É rattled the front door until he got it open and he stumbled out. He headed for the car which was parked in the shade just a few paces away. He touched the door handle but immediately pulled his hand back in pain. The handle was burning hot.

"Owww! Shit!"

He touched the car again and pulled his hand back again. He looked up at the shade, trying to figure it out. Was that shade or did he just imagine that it was shade? He was as confused as he had ever been. What had those bastards put in his drink, anyway?

The house door was still open and music was still pouring out. Suddenly Tzoquito came dancing out, too, still weaving side to side from the angry impulse Jinete had given him. He came over, laughed and flung himself against the car, right next to El É. He embraced the car and rested his cheek on the hood. El É was astonished and tentatively touched the car again. It was as cool as he would expect it to be, there under the tree. He rested his hand on it and then leaned forward on it to talk to Tzoquito. Their speech was slurred but they still managed to make themselves understood.

"I don't get it! A second ago this car was burning hot. Now it's cool."

Tzoquito laughed. In spite of his daze, he understood completely. "That's what you get for fucking with the ancestors!"

"What do you mean?"

"The rocks made it hot," Tzoquito explained. "They're angry. And when they get angry they can burn themselves right down into the Earth with the heat of their vengeance! We're fucked, El É!" He laughed wildly.

El É couldn't figure out what Tzoquito's game was, but he was sure of one thing. "We ain't bringing the rocks back to that old cellar, Tzoquito. We've been waiting for two years for an opportunity like this."

"No, forget about returning them. It's too late for that, now. The rocks are already fired up and furious. They will punish us, you'll see."

He laughed again. El É got as close as he could, resting his face on the car roof next to Tzoquito's.

"So the rocks heated up the car, right?"

Tzoquito nodded with an amused smile.

"So why is it cool now?"

"Because I'm here now," Tzoquito said matter of factly. "They trust me, they know I am from the same place they're from."

El É had to laugh. "You've got a lot of crazy stories, Tzoquito. Where do you get all these stories?"

"Where do you think I get them? From the crazy place I come from." He stopped for a moment and seemed to choke up a bit as he basted self pity onto his words. "I'm a freak, El É, that's all there is to it." His voice had changed to something dramatic.

If it was an act, it was a good one. El É also spoke softer now. After all, he didn't mean any harm. "I didn't mean that you're a freak, man. I think it's interesting."

"But it's not," Tzoquito continued with this successful line. "Not to me. To me it's just sad. Very sad. You know how to do everything. I only know how to be a freak!"

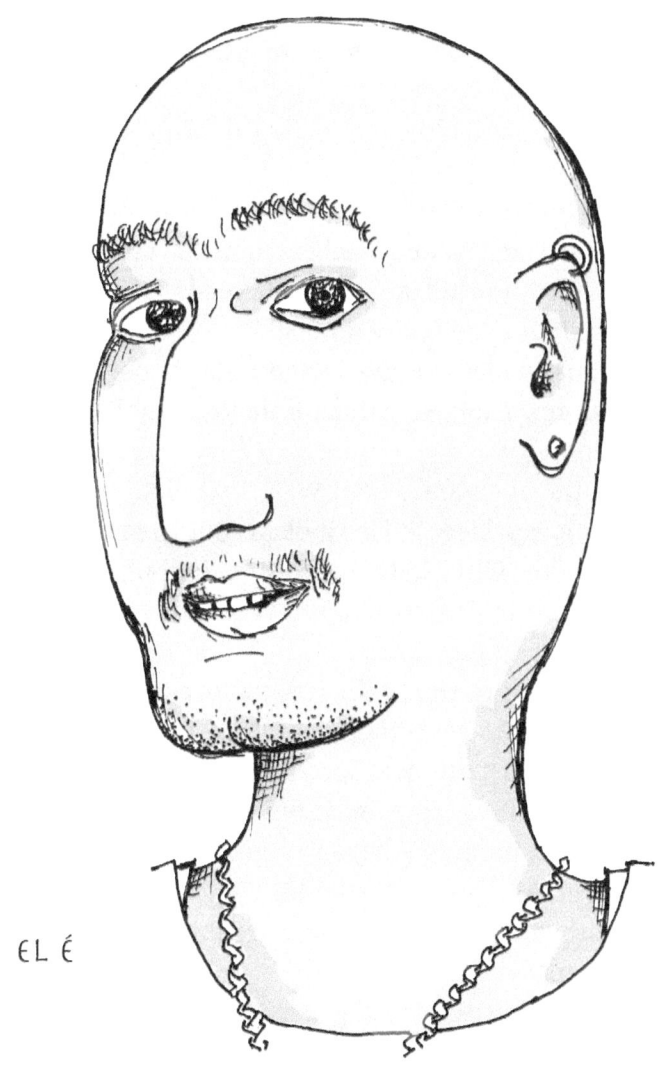

ƐL É

El É laughed nervously and the sound of his laughter seemed to calm the Indian down. Tzoquito changed mood and just like that, the regrets were forgotten. He moved his hands around the car roof and observed the field beyond.

"You know what this reminds me of?" Tzoquito was suddenly remembering, thinking back on another life. "Sometimes on a hot afternoon, I would lie down on a cool rock, high up on a ridge and I would look down at the valley. I loved the cool rocks up there. I would rest my cheek there and open my mouth and lick the rocks for hours."

He opened his mouth and began licking the roof of the car. El É was quick to react.

"Whoa! You *are* a freak!"

Tzoquito stopped and stared back at him as though he would burst into tears. Oh, no, not again. El É made quick amends. "I mean, I'm kidding! Did you really do that?"

"Yes and I would watch the towns and villages below, for hours: Chamula, San Andres, Cielitos. All the little towns and all the people that know everything!"

El É gave a little laugh and said, "Well, I wouldn't say that those hillbillies know *everything!*" He looked out over the field in imitation of Tzoquito. Obviously, he wasn't the only one who had swallowed something in that farmhouse. He was beginning to enjoy hanging with this freaky guy.

"But you know, you're right," El É said. "I can see the villages, too! Right over there – I see Cielitos right over there!"

He pointed at an indeterminate spot in the field. Tzoquito looked carefully, disappointedly seeing only the field. But then when he realized that it was a game, he began to play along. These humans were not so difficult to figure out, after all.

"Yes, it looks beautiful from up here on this cool rock, doesn't it?" Tzoquito dreamed.

"Yeah." El É dreamed, too.

"You know what I'd do next?" Tzoquito continued, so glad to finally have someone to confide in. "If I was all alone? I would sneak on down! Come on, I'll show you!"

He moved back from the car in a crouching position, pulling El É along with him, hand in human hand. After checking with a quick glance to be sure that no one was watching, El É let the skinny little guy lead him by the hand and pull him along, around the car with sneaking steps and hunched backs. They entered the field, binquizac style. As they moved, they hunched closer to the ground until they were practically walking on all fours. They got halfway across the field and then they ended up flat on their stomachs almost hidden in the high grass. El É was laughing, as he extracted his hand from the sweaty grip, but Tzoquito was serious and his voice brought his friend right back to the dream, with an intensity that startled El É.

"I'd sink down into the grass, just like this and I'd lie here and watch the people for hours."

"I thought you lived in a village in the high mountains."

"We lived in the forest. Near Cielitos, or near some of the other towns around there. We lived wherever we liked."

"You watched Cielitos like that?"

"Yes, sometimes. At Cielitos I used to lie on that big rock above Lupe's house."

"You watched Lupe?" El É's voice took on a more alert tone.

Tzoquito hesitated for a moment, then responded. "Yes. Once when she came back from San Cristóbal."

"You know, Tzoquito, you're freakin' with my head."

"I told you! I'm a freak!" Tzoquito said in sudden defeat.

El É didn't like this conversation anymore, but he had to get to the bottom of it. "Why would you just sit on a rock and look at the town, why didn't you just go down into town?"

"I did go into town. But when I was there I had to hide. I used to hide under cars and watch people's feet as they went by all evening."

"Yeah, right, Tzoquito. Now I know you're full of shit."

"You don't understand, El É." He turned to his friend and finally said what he had never said before. "I'm a binquizac! I couldn't talk to anybody, I couldn't even let them see me, or they would run away screaming. Because I'm a fucking binquizac! A freak of nature!"

But El É wasn't buying it and he was getting irritated. "I don't believe in binquizacs, Tzoquito. You're just Tzoquito. And you're a liar and a fucking stalker, too. You're just as psycho as that little pig Kweeche."

They looked at each other, each at a loss for words, unwilling to move this dangerous conversation one step further. Then they turned back to watch the field for awhile, each to his own thoughts.

Suddenly there was a commotion back at the house. It was Kweeche's voice, with his porcine squeal.

"Owwww! What the fuck!"

They crawled back to a spot where they could see while still remaining hidden in the foliage. Kweeche was standing by the Chevy waving his burnt hand in the air. He kicked the car. Next to him were two of his men. They were looking around but they didn't see El É and Tzoquito in the tall grass.

"Goddamn piece of shit car!" Kweeche shouted, screeching like his cousin.

Pinto, Brolo and Jinete came tumbling out of the house, being pushed forward by a couple of goons.

"Hey, cousin, what the hell are you doin'?" Pinto said.

"Don't give me that cousin shit," Kweeche said in a high pitched rasp. "What have you got in this car? There's a big box in there! I know you're here just waiting till dark, when the cops will be too drunk and too tired to stop you. Come on, Pinto! You give us some of that action and I'll see that you get through. I got some guys on the back porch right now who can arrange everything."

"I don't know what you're talking about, man" Pinto said, his voice also getting higher. "We stopped here for a rest and a good time. Don't fuck it all up now."

"Listen, you amateurs are about as cool as a bunch of First Communion girls at confession. It's written all over your faces. And I'm tryin' to be nice!" He turned nervously to his goons. "Ain't I tryin' to be nice, men?"

One of his goons nodded solemnly, trying to figure out if First Communion girls are supposed to be cool. The other one stayed a bit more focused and answered agreeably. "You're tryin' to be nice," he stated.

Suitably encouraged, Kweeche turned back to the occupants of the car, "But you're pushing me too far. Now open up this car and show me what you got, or I'm gonna fuckin' smash the windows!"

"Hey, that's not cool, man," Brolo said, as he took a cautious step closer to the mean little Kweeche. El É and Tzoquito got to their feet on shaky legs. Pinto saw them now standing in the grass a few yards away and he called out.

"Hey, El É, let's get the fuck out of here! This ain't right. Jinete! Let's get our shit, man, we're getting out of here. This is insulting!"

Jinete and Pinto disappear into the house, not waiting for anyone to object.

Inside the storm-tossed living room, Jinete and Pinto started quickly gathering up shirts and hats dead-set on making a hasty escape. Jinete went to the coffee table and grabbed an empty plastic envelope, the kind used for retail quantities of powdery drugs. He held it up to Pinto.

"I know how to get through that roadblock and teach that little Indian fuck a good lesson, all in one shot!"

Then he went over to a tray of dirty coffee cups and found a sugar cube. He put the sugar cube into the envelope and banged it down on the table with his fist, smashing the contents. He held it up again for Pinto to see, this time containing a half crushed cube of sugar and some loose crystals.

"Huh?" Pinto said. "That's just a sugar cube! Anybody can see that from a mile away!"

"Not if you're a cop that's been standing out in the sun for too long! Let's do it!" Jinete said.

Pinto didn't say anything, as he was barely listening. He had to concentrate on his own helter-skelter actions trying to gather their few but scattered possessions in order to get the hell out of this place. When they got to the doorway, they stopped in dismay. It was clear that things were getting even further out of hand.

A scuffle had broken out next to the car. Kweeche pushed Brolo back and tried to touch the car handle once again. He shouted in pain. Kweeche's bodyguards stood crowded around, watching the spectacle. They were apparently more for show than for any actual muscle.

"Get back out here, Pinto, you lousy fuck!" Kweeche shouted. "What's with this goddamn car, anyway?"

"It's got a special alarm system to keep low-life assholes like you away from it!" El É said, with coolness that seemed at odds with his hostile words. It was the attitude of invulnerability. He was standing fully in Kweeche's face.

"What, do you think I'm gonna believe that?" Kweeche asked. But from his cautious tone, it was clear that El É's confidence had had its desired effect. "I ain't no *poblano* from the hills, *perro.*" Kweeche finished, as though to convince himself, as well.

One of the goons touched the car and pulled back sharply .

"Let's get out of here!" Pinto said, seizing the moment... And seizing the handle, as well. But he too had to jump back. "Holy shit! He's right!" he exclaimed. Everyone was stumped, on both sides and they all stepped back a bit, eyeing each other and trying to anticipate the others' next moves.

El É took a quick look at Tzoquito to make sure he was conscious and ready to move. Then he spoke. What the hell? He had nothing to lose and if by some crazy chance it worked, it would be their ticket out of there.

"Let Tzoquito go first, then," El É said. "He knows how to deactivate it."

No one said anything, so Tzoquito walked up to the car and opened the back door without hesitation. After that, before anyone else had time to react, El É opened the driver's door and motioned Pinto to open the other back door.

"You see?" El É said out loud. "It just takes the touch of an honest man. Like the fairy tale says!"

"Fuck you and all your fairies and all their fucking tails!" Kweeche said, recovering a bit from his surprise. "Is this the way you pay me back for my hospitality? You *pendejos* aren't worth shit. Now, tell me, what's in that box?"

Brolo, who was not known for his intelligence, took this moment to open the trunk to put his jacket in there. Kweeche looked over and saw the other six boxes. Brolo realized his mistake too late and hurriedly closed the trunk and jumped into the car. Kweeche tried to get to the trunk, but Pinto managed to get in the way, as the others hurried into the car.

And as Tzoquito got in, Jinete slipped the envelope into the back pocket of Tzoquito's jeans.

"It was great to see you, cousin!" Pinto was saying, as he pulled his cousin slack wristed and confused through a whole series of handshake moves. Kweeche wasn't good at multi-tasking and so he resigned himself to the farewell ritual and momentarily forgot all else. "My mother is visiting your mother next week!" Pinto lied, just to keep him focused. "I'll call and tell them I saw you." He jumped into the back.

El É took a long, grateful look at Tzoquito in the rear view mirror, as though finally understanding who he was dealing with. Then with everyone inside, he turned the ignition and sped off.

"Fuck you!" Kweeche shouted in their dust.

"Don't worry about it," said one of Kweeche's goons. "They won't get very far. We'll get a couple of the boys to go down that way to Cielitos. We'll see what they've got and we'll get our share. You can depend on that."

"Okay," Kweeche answered. Then he mumbled so no one else could hear, "but take it easy. My mamma would kill me if anything happened to my stupid cousin."

8

Back on the open blacktop road, it didn't take long for the Chevy to reach the troublesome hill. El É slowed down as the car approached the incline and it came to a full stop halfway up, where it still would not be seen from the other side.

"The roadblock should be just over the hill," Pinto said. "That's where they always set it up." They were in his part of Mexico now. "Jinete's got a plan for running it."

"El È, go check out if they've got the road totally blocked off," Jinete said forcefully.

Now this was too much. "Since when am I the lookout?" El É responded, just as forcefully.

"What, are you going to trust *them* to do it?" he nodded to indicate the backseaters. "And I've got my plan, so I gotta stay right here. So just do it, man. My plan is gonna work!"

El É got out and started walking on the road. Jinete called out. "Get down!"

El É crouched down and started walking along the dirt shoulder of the road, getting lower as he reached the crest, much as he had been walking with Tzoquito earlier. He reached the top. From there he could see the whole expanse of road for a long distance. But he didn't have to see very far; just 200 feet down the hill were two cop cars parked on either side of the road. Four policemen were leaning against the cars, talking and drinking beer from bottles.

He looked back at the Chevy to let them know that the roadblock was there, but he could see that the occupants weren't even watching him anymore. He got the feeling that Jinete had sent him out just to get rid of him.

Inside the car, Jinete had turned around to the back as soon as El É had gotten a few steps away. "Tzoquito, you know who the police are?" he asked.

"Yes, Lupe's neighbors were talking about them. They are people that can solve everything!"

Jinete couldn't contain a laugh. "You got it! They can solve everything. You've got to distract them for us. Why don't you go and ask them a question that you want answered, so we can drive by. Then we'll pick you up down the road."

"You mean me go alone?" Tzoquito didn't like the sound of that.

"Yeah! What are you afraid of?" Jinete insisted. "You know you've got to prove yourself if you're gonna hang with the boyz. And you know the police can solve anything, so go ask them something you want to know."

"Hey, quit it man!" Brolo said. He didn't know what Jinete was getting at, but he didn't like the way he was teasing Tzoquito.

Pinto took up Jinete's part. "Shut up, Brolo! Tzoquito, ask them who does Lupe really love: you or El É!"

"No, man!" Brolo insisted. "Tzoquito, don't do it."

But Tzoquito wasn't listening to Brolo. Jinete's talk about hanging with the boyz was still resonating in his head. Really, he didn't mind doing something, if it was going to help him prove himself.

"Would they really know the answer to that?"

"Yes, of course!" Pinto said, wondering where did this kid come from, anyway. Then Pinto opened his door to let Tzoquito out, just as El É got back in.

"They're just down the hill," El É reported. "Do you really think we can drive right through, now? Before it gets dark? Is that your big master plan?"

Then he noticed Tzoquito getting out of the car. "Now where is he going?"

"He's our decoy," Jinete said smartly. "They'll be so occupied with him, they won't even notice us coming through."

"That's bullshit!" El É said. "Right away they'll see that he's stoned on something and give him a hard time."

"Especially when they find the bag of white powder that Jinete stashed in his back pocket!" Pinto squeaked.

"Shut up, fuck face!" Jinete shouted.

"You son of a bitch, Jinete!" El É said.

"Calm down, El É, that little Indian can take care of himself! Those fat cops will be chasing him all night the way that little dog runs."

"*¡Chinga a tu madre,* Jinete!" El É said as he jumped out of the car and started after Tzoquito.

"Tzoquito!" he called out, as loud as he dared.

"*¡Cállate, cabrón!"* Jinete called out to his leader. This was out and out rebellion now.

But El É ignored him. "Tzoquito!" he called again but Tzoquito didn't turn back. "Tzoquito!" he insisted, just as he reached him at the crest of the hill. But it was too late. El É grabbed Tzoquito to stop him right there at the crest, in full view of the cops, who lazily watched the scene unfold, with their bottles in their fists.

"Come back, little brother!" El É said out loud as he pulled Tzoquito backwards. "Those fuckers set you up."

"No, let me do it, El É! I want to help out, too!"

El É started checking Tzoquito's pockets frantically.

"What are you doing? Stop it!" Tzoquito protested.

"They put a bag of coke in your pocket!" El É explained. "Right there!" he said, as he found the little plastic bag in Tzoquito's back pocket. He held it up to Tzoquito's face without even noticing that it was only sugar. "*¡Drogas!*" he explained to the uncomprehending Indian.

He threw it away on the road. The cops looked at each other and reluctantly won over their stupor and started running up the hill.

"Hey, you two! Come here!" one of them called.

El É and Tzoquito looked down at the cops running toward them. El É took Tzoquito's arm to pull him to the right to start running through the downhill field on their side of the hill. They would be able to catch the car down a ways, if the guys turned back. They went a few steps and the cops started to follow them off the road. El É's move had only succeeded in giving the cops a short cut to avoid chugging up to the crest.

"No, wait! This way!" Tzoquito said, changing course. Tzoquito pulled back on El É and pulled him with such inhuman force that El É had no choice but to come with him. And he brought him back up to the road, across it and up the slope of the mountain on the other side, toward the trees.

The cops stopped, cursed out loud and then crossed over to chase them now up the hill.

"Ay! What are you doing, Tzoquito?" El É shouted. "We'll never get back to the car this way."

Pinto and Brolo were already out of the car and cautiously approaching the crest to see what was happening. When they saw their two friends running up the hillside instead of back to the car, with the cops right behind them, they waved at Jinete to bring the car forward.

"Come on, Jinete! Drive! We can get through!" Pinto shouted.

Brolo was not ready to give up on El É and Tzoquito, though. He ran to the top of road and looked at the fleeing twosome.

"El É! Hey! We're over here!"

But it was no use. Tzoquito and El É were already making their way far out of earshot, with the four cops stumbling up the slope after them.

"Fuck El É!" Jinete snarled, as he pulled up in the car and came to a stop. "Either we get through now or we don't! Get in the car, *pendejos!*"

Pinto jumped in the car. "Come on, Brolo!" he shouted, "We'll find them on the other side of the mountain, somewhere." But Brolo wasn't listening. Now he was running around in circles on the crest of the hill, looking down at the asphalt.

"What the hell are you doing, man?" Pinto asked.

"I'm looking for the bag of coke!" he said frantically. "Shit! Why'd he have to throw it down without lookin' what he was doin?"

"It was granulated sugar!" Jinete screamed. "Get in, *pendejo*, or I'll leave your ass right here!"

And the *pendejo* obeyed.

They sped over the hill and passed easily right between the two unattended cop cars. Brolo craned his neck up, to follow the action on the mountainside. He was just in time to see Tzoquito pull El É into a bunch of bushes, where just the tops of their heads were visible. By now the two of them were moving inhumanly fast. They just reached the first trees of the forest with the cops in hopeless, widening pursuit.

"Stop! Stop! You bastards!" One of the cops shouted, as they slowed down, coming to realize that they were never going to catch these two. They slowed to a walk and then to a complete stop when one of them started pointing furiously back down at the road behind them.

A car was speeding past their roadblock. They looked at each other, not sure what to do. The only thing for sure was that they had been tricked.

"Hey!" the fourth cop called out drunkenly to the car. Then he shot twice recklessly at the speeding car, but missed into the wide open air.

"Shit! There's nothing we can do about that now," his partner said. "Come on, we'll get these two!"

These two cops began again to run uphill, while the other two remained in place. No need for everyone to follow the same strategy, was there? And in any case, the two delinquents had by now completely disappeared into the trees.

"No! Wait!," one of the running cops said, huffing for breath. "Can't you see? It's an ambush! What do you think will happen when we get close enough to those trees for them to shoot? We'll all be dead! Let them go! We'll radio in a description of the car and they'll catch them further down the road."

All the cops jumped at his words, suddenly aware of the danger and thankful for an excuse to put an end to all this strenuous activity. They slowly limped back downhill toward their cars.

"Good thinking, compadre!" one of the other cops said. "Who got a good look at that car? I think it was a white SUV."

"No," said the first cop. "It was more like a lime green! And it looked more like one of those stretch limousines."

Meanwhile the blue Chevy Impala put long, clean distance between itself and the roadblock. The three occupants, Jinete at the wheel and the two remaining soldiers in back, could once again take a deep breath and try to relax. Brolo took that breathe but he didn't relax. In fact, the first thing that he did after that was turn to his seatmate Pinto and give him a solid fisted punch right in the lip.

"Fuck!" the other squeaked in pain. "What'd you do that for?!" He whined, though he knew damn well.

Deep in the forest, Tzoquito and El É were running at ballistic speeds through the trees and bushes. Branches and twigs bent and snapped away all around them as though cutting a path for them right through the thick growth.

"Stop! Stop, Tzoquito! Stop!" El É shouted, for about the tenth time.

Tzoquito stopped and let go of El É's armpit, the hold that Tzoquito had been using to pull him along. El É collapsed on the ground in a small clearing and Tzoquito stopped and collapsed back down with him. A flutter of little nightbirds rose up and then down, resettling around them.

"Damn, we've been running for miles!" El É said between gasps for air. We must have lost those cops a half hour ago!"

"That's okay," Tzoquito answered, not the least bit winded. This way we will be back in Cielitos in the morning."

"Cielitos? But that must be another fifty miles from here!"

"Not over the mountain," the former forest creature responded coolly. "Come and look!"

Tzoquito started crawling on all fours over to a nearby ridge where he scampered up atop the outcropping of huge boulders. El É followed him on all fours, far less nimbly and with a fraction of the energy. He pulled himself up slowly onto the rocks, his every step anticipated by the nightbirds, which alit and flew repeatedly, marking the points of his path. Once up on the rocks, he breathed in deep, there to see an immense, panoramic view of the land below.

"Look over there, beyond that low hill is the valley of Cielitos," Tzoquito said. "It's not far at all."

"You're fucking amazing, Tzoquito. But there's only one problem. I can't move forward another inch."

"That's okay. we'll sleep here and go on in the morning."

"Out here?" the Angelino responded. "You're crazy! With all the wild animals? They'll eat us alive!"

"Don't worry about the animals," Tzoquito answered, proud to be the one in the know this time. "They will treat us like guests. They are much better hosts than Pinto's cousin Kweeche."

El É had to laugh at that thought. "Well, I don't think we were very good guests, either!"

Now they both laughed. El É looked out at the panorama, resting his chin on the massive stone, just as Tzoquito was doing, just as they had practiced earlier that afternoon. "It is a beautiful, peaceful place here," El É said, with a warmth Tzoquito hadn't before heard in his voice. "Far away from the people. And look at the sunset; you can never see it like this in the valley."

"That's because the nighttime rises from the bottom of the valley and covers the town first. Up here we are above the night."

"No, Tzoquito, night time comes down from the dark sky. They say 'night falls'"

Tzoquito laughed again. "They say that because they don't really know. Watch from here, El É and and you will see the nighttime. You'll see it seep up from the deepest point, from the wells and downstream from the lowland woods. It doesn't fall from the sky, — it never even reaches the sky, because the great bowl of the sky stands watch over the great bowl of the valley all night long. The

people and the animals, they invented the nighttime so they can sleep. The sky never sleeps."

El É rolled over on his back and looked up at the sky, where the stars were just beginning to twinkle. Tzoquito continued more softly, hypnotically. And as he spoke, El É saw.

"As the land gets darker, look at how the stars brighten up, keeping watch over the people. They watch the people. But tell me, El É, why don't the people ever look back up at them?"

"I don't know," El É mumbled as he struggled to use his voice from the deep and deepening state he was in.

"Let the stars see your face, compadre," Tzoquito continued. "Let the stars color your skin. They have waited a long time to see your face again. They have waited centuries for you to look up again."

El É looked at the brightening stars with a feeling of euphoria that welled up inside of him and seeped up onto his face. Truly, this was a magical place and this Tzoquito was appropriate company. Then satisfied and secure, he closed his eyes and went sliding comfortably further down into a deep sleep. Tzoquito smiled and closed his eyes and did the same.

****

Black turned to red. The sun must have come up, Tzoquito thought. The darkness around him was now a bright, flaming red, as sunlight backlit his closed eyelids. Then came a soft voice, speaking to him in the homeliest language.

"Come back, Tzoquito!"

And the words made Tzoquito ache. He answered in his deepest mind. *"No, I don't know if I can!"*

"Come back, you are in danger there with those people."

Tzoquito realized it was his brother Tepiltzin. *"What do you mean?"*

"They are not your friends, they will hurt you! They have already hurt you. They are bad."

"No, you're wrong, my brother," he immediately protested, as he always did with Tepiltzin. But then he thought again and realized that he could never keep the truth from his brother, there was no point to that. *"Yes, alright, some are bad, but some are good. I will learn the difference."*

"You are too stubborn, little brother. But you are wise and getting wiser every day. So stay if you must. But know this: I won't go away, as long as you are down there with those people. And neither will the others. We are all gathered here, hundreds of us Tzoquito! We are watching everything that happens and we will protect you."

"Thank you, but I don't need your help."

"We are here just the same. If you need us you just have to call out and we will descend like a tornado on those that would hurt you."

****

There was a bright blue sky, cloudless, flawless blue. It was fringed by a border of beautiful, deep green leaves on high branches. Sunlight warmed El É's face, life-giving light from the great loving orb just now floating over the horizon. El É blinked his eyes and looked away from the bright sky. He saw Tzoquito lying next to him, gazing with melancholy at the still sleepy valley spread out below them.

"Who were you talking to?" he asked.

Tzoquito looked at him with surprise. "Me? Nobody."

But El É persisted. "Somebody said that they are here, they won't hurt you, something. I couldn't really understand, I don't know a lot of Mexican words. Come to think of it, I don't know any! It's amazing that I understood anything at all."

"It was just a prayer I say sometimes," Tzoquito said distantly. He seemed so sadly pensive this morning. "You should learn some more of your language. Without that you will never understand what I say, ever, no matter how well I translate it."

"I have enough trouble with Spanish and English. I don't need Mexican, too."

"Believe me, you would have less trouble with other people's languages if you knew your own first."

"Like you with Spanish!"

"I have nothing to fear from these other languages, nothing to fear from the Conquistadores of Spanish or the gringos of English, whoever they are. Their words can't damage me because I am already who I am. I am Mexican, I am from this earth, from this rock and all the languages and customs and pretty things from the world can pop up all around me like summer flowers. I will smell them, I will taste them, I will plant them and let them grow but I will always be here, the earth itself beneath their roots. I will always be me."

El È smiled. "You're right, Tzoquito, when you know your own shit, you won't ever get burned by other people's tricks. I saw that on the way down here from L.A., people with their fake gurus, when their own traditions have the answers, right there under their own noses. The fake guru even tells them that, tells them that he is bullshit, but you know what? They still believe in him, anyway."

"So you are still learning things, too?" Tzoquito asked, just now realizing.

"Yes, of course, Tzoquito. I want to keep learning till the day I die. But it takes courage, you have to walk into all kinds of dangerous places. You know that. That's what I like about you, Tzoquito. You are not afraid of walking into anything. You are a courageous little guy."

That meant a lot to Tzoquito, coming from El É, for the fact was that just as El É was beginning to appreciate the depth of the Indian, this Indian was beginning to understand this townsman from the North and seeing where his truth lay beyond the reach of his folly. He understood that there was something very genuine in this person and he valued El É's judgment deeply.

"Do you really think I'm courageous? I'm surprised you would say that, after I got so scared by those rocks."

"Ah, forget the rocks. Those freaky things could spook anybody. You were the man, yesterday! Do you realize that you got us out of a jam three times? First you got the old couple to run away from the house, then you got the doors open to get us away from Kweeche and then you got us through the roadblock! You're like Batman, or something!"

"A bat?" Tzoquito was dubious, not seeing any connection. "But, you know, there were things that I was very afraid of in Cielitos. I was afraid that you would hurt Lupe. And I was afraid that maybe I cared about her just to try to keep you away. I'm not afraid of any of those things anymore."

Once again, El É neglected to get jealous at Tzoquito's inappropriate interest in Lupe. It was as though he welcomed Tzoquito not as a rival but as some kind of alter ego who could help him find his way with her. He shrugged and said, "Lupe herself will know the right decision. We should let her make her choice."

Tzoquito nodded and the two clasp hands in agreement, with El É bringing him through a few of the moves he had seen the day before.

"But right now we should concentrate on getting home" El É worried. He grabbed his own shirtfront and twisted the cloth over his stomach. "And getting something to eat. I can't even think anymore from hunger!"

The former forest creature looked around. "Well, we could find some things right here among the bushes."

El É gave him a look of profound disappointment. It was not lost on Tzoquito. "Or maybe not," he corrected himself. "I guess we should get down to the valley and get some food there."

"I don't think that's gonna work, either," El É said shamefully. "I lost every dollar in my wallet to Kweeche in that poker game."

****

It's hard to cut chicken or tortilla with the side of a plastic fork, but they tried it anyway. Three plastic forks sawing fiercely at the outdoor meal, as three plastic knives lay clean and untouched on the plastic table.

The three homeys were sitting at the one wobbly table set up next to a roadside foodstand, devouring their breakfast of tortillas and chicken. The car was parked nearby, heating up the shade under a big tree. Jinete and Brolo were munching contentedly. Pinto was chewing very, very carefully, trying to avoid too much pain in his cut lip and swollen cheek where Brolo had punched him.

"Do you think there's a bus station around here somewhere?" Brolo asked. "Maybe we could find them at some bus station."

"Forget it!" Jinete said. "We've been driving around looking here, waiting there all night! We're not going to find them by just driving around half of Mexico."

"He's right," Pinto said. "Yeah, we fucked up, but we're not going to make it any better by hanging around here, waiting to come up to another roadblock."

Brolo knew they were right, so he kept his mouth shut. When they were done, Jinete paid the vendor and then looked over at the car with disgust. A haze of shimmering heated air all around the car reminded him of what they were in for.

"Come on, hombres. We're in a hurry. Don't even think about it!" he said like a commander to his troops and he walked briskly back to the car, followed by Brolo and the sheepish Pinto. Each of them stopped at a door: Jinete at the driver's door and the two others at the back. Each of them took off his shirt and wrapped it around one hand in order to touch the car door handle. They quickly opened up the doors and hopped in, careful to avoid the metal frame.

BROLO

Jinete turned the key in a hurry and exclaimed as he shook his fingers afterwards. Then they drove away with their arms at their sides, eyeing the chrome trim on the door handles next to them with trepidation. Further up the road, the roadside sign said 40 kilometers to Cielitos. It would be a hot hot hot ride back to town.

The vendor watched all this with wonder. And relief. He was glad to see the big hot Chevy disappear along the road, even if it was probably the last customer of the morning. Now, maybe the stand would cool back down a bit. He scraped at the pots that had served day laborers and market goers since before sunrise. He covered up one, then another kerosene cooker and began to think about the long haul of pots back to his house, to pick up the food his wife was now preparing for the evening return.

But as it turned out, the hot Chevy boys were not the last customers of the morning. Fifteen minutes later, just as he was about to leave, he had some more. This time, a cop car with four cops inside. Two cops stepped out, stretched their legs painfully and limped over to the vendor.

"Hey, amigo! Any business today?" the cop with the big belly said.

The vendor nodded suspiciously. A question like that could only mean trouble. "Maybe." he said and quickly added, "Just enough to pay a bill or two."

The cop ignored him. He was looking around, at the stand, at the ground and at the view, as though he were acting in some cop film. This was something new, the vendor thought and could only mean even more trouble.

"You can see a whole stretch of the mountain from here."

"What?" the vendor asked. The cop ignored him.

"What's that mountain called?" the cop asked in a false sounding conversational tone. The vendor stared at him like stone, wondering what he could possibly mean. Then the cop huffed with exasperation and just came out with it.

"Did you see two guys come down from the forest this morning?"

"No. What two guys?" the vendor asked.

"Young guys. *Cholos*. On drugs," he said dramatically .

"Come down from the forest on foot?"

"Yes!" the cop answered impatiently. This vendor was a bit slow. "They got away from us last night."

The vendor laughed. So they were investigating something! "No, I didn't see anyone like that. I only saw some young guys in a car. They stopped for breakfast."

The cops in the car perked up. One of them stuck his head out. "What kind of car was it?"

Oh, shit, the vendor thought. Why did he have to go and tell them that? "I don't know. I don't interest myself in cars. I just know it was hot."

"A hot car? Stolen?" the cop said.

"No," his partner chided, hitting his arm. "He means hot, like it was an expensive import car or something. Maybe a lime green limosine."

The first cop pushed him away and looked back at the vendor. "Did they really steal your car?"

"No!" the vendor said, with irritation. "The car was hot, like temperature hot! It was so hot they could hardly touch it."

That didn't make any sense, so the cops didn't bother to follow up. "Was it a white car? A big white car?" one cop asked.

"No, it was blue," the vendor said.

"Was it green? Some kind of a green car?" another cop asked.

"No. it was blue."

"That's it! It was a blue car!" the first cop said. "It was blue-white! It was a white car, just like I said last night!"

"No, it was green. Blue, green, it's almost the same thing!" his buddy argued.

From inside the car, an angry police voice shouted. "Shut up! Find out where they were going!"

"Where were they going?" the first cop said angrily to the vendor, passing the sergeant's irritation on to him.

"I don't know. But they asked how far it was to Cielitos de Chiapas from here."

"Cielitos de Chiapas! That's not far at all!"

"Let's go!"

The two cops jumped back into the car and they sped off.

"Without buying anything," the vendor nodded ruefully. "Maybe I should have told him the name of that damned mountain."

9

At just about the same time, two dusty figures walked into the town of Cielitos. They were exhausted, dirty, their clothes were ragged and torn, but they were extremely happy to be home, even though neither one had ever thought of this place as home before.

They stopped in front of the Meléndez house. "Lupe! Lupe!" El É called out.

He called again. After a few moments, Lupe came to the upstairs balcony and looked down.

"El É! And Tzoquito! What are you shouting about?" But they were too exhausted to answer.

"I'll be right there!" she said and she hurried back inside behind the white embroidered curtain. Moments later she reappeared at the front door. "¡Ay, Dios mio! You both look terrible! What happened?"

"Nothing!" El É said, not wishing to dramatize for the female and all of her neighbors. "We just ran clear across the state of Chiapas, that's all, right through the forest!"

"Oh, that's horrible!"

"No, it was fun!" Tzoquito said proudly.

"Well, it was okay. or, actually, it was fun!" El É said, just now realizing that this was true. "Anyway, can we clean ourselves up in your garden? I don't want to go home like this." As Lupe stared at his ripped and dirty clothes, he added, "and Tzoquito still doesn't know what to say to Don José."

"Go ahead! Sit down in the shade there by the garden spigot. I'll get some soap and towels."

"And get some food, too," El É called.

El É and Tzoquito went around to the side and entered her "garden" where planters made from old tires and paint cans had transformed a concrete alleyway between the houses into a verdant refuge of fragrant herbs, flowers and vines. They sat on a cement bench and waited peacefully. They sat together wordlessly, having reached a point where conversation was no longer necessary. Lupe returned with a basin for water and two towels. She filled the basin from the spigot and sat down to watch as her two suitors squatted down by the water and washed their faces, necks and arms and at the same time ate the fruit and peppers and tortilla she had put together in the kitchen. When they held their hands out, she handed them the towels.

"Why did you come back through the forest?" she asked, but they didn't answer, with their mouths stuffed with food. However, at this point, she felt she had a right to know, so she persisted. "Were you two in trouble?"

The two laughed.

"Trouble? No trouble at all," El É said, not even bothering to sound convincing. "We just got lost. Really lost. We lost everything and everybody! And it was great! We came back with empty pockets but content with the world."

Lupe scrutinized El É. She didn't know what to make of all this.

"There is something different about you two. I don't know what it is. It's only been one day and two nights, but it seems like you've been gone a long time. Like I'm seeing you after a very long time."

"A very long time!" Tzoquito agreed.

El É high fived him. Tzoquito reciprocated clumsily and with a laugh.

The thumping sound of hip hop music was abruptly bouncing off the walls and getting louder. Suddenly it became very loud and they turned to look out at the street. A car came rumbling along the road, around the curve and past the garden. A purple-hot Chevy.

"El É, isn't that your car?" Lupe asked.

"Yeah. I don't care, let them have their fun. I don't want to talk to them right now."

Lupe waved her hand in front of her face. "Uff! It must be overheating! What a blast of heat came off of that car. And what a stink, too!"

Tzoquito and El É looked at each other. "Those stones must be damn mad now!" El É said.

In a moment they were laughing like teenagers. Rolling-on-the-floor- LMAO-laughing.

The purple-hot Chevy pulled up to the gate at Jinete's house. In the back seat, Pinto wrapped his tee shirt around the inside door handle, popped open the door and jumped out. He went over to the gate and swung it open, thankful to be out of that burning crate of metal and back on cool mother earth. Jinete drove through, still sitting cautiously pulled in all to himself in the car.

Once inside, Jinete and Brolo also got out. They were all wet with sweat and as they wiped the perspiration off their faces and necks, they realized they were not alone. They were surrounded by three thugs they had never seen before. And thug number one was pointing a gun menacingly right at them.

"Get away from the car!" he commanded.

Jinete took a step away, but only one. This was, after all, his own yard and he wasn't going to be pushed around so easily.

"What do you want with us?" he said back, with a gangsta flick of his head. But the thug was unimpressed.

"Don't worry, pretty boy, we don't want you. We just want what's in the car."

"There's nothing in the car," Pinto said.

"Yeah, that's what you keep saying," the other thug said. "So I guess you don't mind if we keep whatever we find."

"My own fucking cousin! What a bastard!" Pinto said with a showy, saliva-less spit.

"Forget about your stinkin' little cousin, Napoleon!" the first thug said, trying the same saliva-less spit – unsuccessfully, as a bit of dribble ran down his cheek. "He ain't gonna hear shit about this. It's between you and us now. So get away from the car!"

Brolo got away from the car. It was way too hot there, anyway. "Shit, man, let them have the boxes, it ain't worth dying over."

Thugs number two and three looked at each other. This was all the confirmation they needed. They moved on the car from both sides. They both grabbed car doors but then immediately cried out in pain, their

TWO THUGS

hands still stuck to the burning metal. The car was really heating up now, as though its rocks were stoking up for a real fight. Thug number one went running to them, to figure out what was going on. But when he tried to pull his friend's hand off the car, he got burned, too and fell against the door. He started jumping around, like a drop of water on a hot skillet and his pistol went flying far away and onto the ground.

The three homeys took this as their cue to grab the thugs and push them up against the car, leaning into them with all their might and making them get a good feel for this Chevy. Their shouts of pain was enough to bring the whole neighborhood to their balconies and the smell of their porky flesh and the shouts from their throats swirled in the air. It was like riding broncos, though, as the big lugs bounced around on the metal car. The three homeys only held them down for a few seconds before they were thrown off. But a few seconds was long enough and each of the thugs ended up bouncing away harmlessly, concerned only with holding themselves together and rolling on the ground to cool off.

"Come on! Let's go!" Jinete said and he jumped back in the car. "Pinto, get in! Brolo, get the gate!"

As Pinto jumped in and Brolo fumbled with the gate to get it back open again, another car went rushing by. The cops. Brolo saw it but was so panicky, it didn't even register who it was.

Just like it didn't register to any of them that the Chevy was no longer superheated and no longer purple and that they had gotten in without burning themselves. The boxes were on their side now.

There was a screech of tires in front of Lupe's house. Cops number three and four jumped out of the back seat and looked around. Neighbors on the usual terraces called down to them. "They're in there! In her garden!" the next door neighbor shouted. It seemed everybody in the whole town was watching now.

Lupe, Tzoquito and El É got up to see what was going on, just as the two cops entered the garden. Without thinking, the two boys imagined that maybe they could get away unseen, so they turned and ran toward the back wall of the garden.

But it was too late. Cop number three was already right there and had spotted them trying to flee. He trotted back out to the street and waved over the other two, still in the car. "Come on! We've got'em cornered in there!" he shouted.

But just as the two front seat cops were getting out, another car came up behind them in the narrow road. The three homeys, driving wildly up the street. They slammed on the brakes and just barely avoided rear-ending the cop car.

The front seat cops recognized the car – blue, green, limousine, whatever it was. They pointed at it, speechless and Jinete threw the car into reverse and started speeding backwards back down the street.

The two cops started dancing around like Keystone Kops, not sure whether to give chase on foot or with the car. Who wanted to make a U-turn in this narrow side-street, anyway? But they were interrupted by the voices from the garden.

Cop number four, who had not seen the Chevy, couldn't believe that these clowns were still standing around the cop car, now hopping around like idiots. "Move it, *flojos!*" he shouted in anger. "They're gonna get away!"

So the front seat cops gave up on the getaway car and ran into the alley garden.

Meanwhile, the Chevy was still speeding backwards, a skill that Jinete still had to get the hang of. At a certain point it started swerving first one way and then the other and then at a slight curve in the road, it went totally out of control. Jinete ended up sending the Chevy crashing backwards into his neighbor's wooden chicken house. It disappeared inside with a loud boom.

A boom so loud, in fact, that the front seat cops heard it echo around them, just as they were about to enter the garden. They both threw themselves to the ground on the sidewalk.

"They're shooting at us!" cop number one shouted.

"Where's it coming from?" his partner asked. "One of these windows?" He looked up and saw the faces of all the neighbors staring down at him with scorn.

"No!" one old lady said. And she pointed at the garden. "Keep going!"

They looked in the alley where they saw Cop number three struggling with EL É and Cop number four on the ground holding onto Tzoquito's ankle. He was being dragged along as Tzoquito tried to crawl away.

"Come on, *pendejos!* Help us out!" one of the struggling cops called back to them.

And the four cops finally subdued the two young men.

Back at the chicken house, Jinete, Pinto and Brolo came running out of the pile of rotted wood, in a cloud of feathers and hay. They were met by the three thugs, who were running up too, waving their arms in front of their faces to ward off the hysterical chickens that were flying around in every direction.

"You bastards! You tricked us!" the first thug said. "We were only trying to scare you and you went nuts! You burnt my cheek! You're gonna pay for that!"

The thugs threw themselves on top of the three homeys to wrestle them to the ground, but the poor thugs were exhausted and in excruciating pain from their burns. Just touching them was enough to set them howling and they were thus easily bested by even these scrawny wannabes. But there were even more problems to come. The boxed-up stone-carved occupants in the Chevy's trunk had gotten angry again. Red hot angry and now the chicken shed was smoking up, unnoticed behind them. Suddenly there was another loud boom, this time as the whole ramshackle heap of dry wood and hay burst into flames. Everyone stopped rolling around to stare.

"Oh my God! All that good weed!" thug number three said.

Jinete and Pinto just looked at each other and laughed. Weed? These guys were as clueless as everyone else.

Back at Lupe's the other wrestling had also ended, with the cops firmly in control of the two young men. Now that they had them down, albeit squirming in their grip, they tried to figure out what would come next. Now why exactly were they chasing them again?

"Ummm. Because they ran away?" one cop ventured.

"Because they threw something down on the road!" another one interjected, a bit more decidedly.

Then they heard the boom of the exploding chicken shed.

"Ay, Chihuahua!" cop number three said. "They're shooting at us again!"

"Who's shooting at you?" El É asked, but the cop had no answer. This whole thing was getting too complicated for a man in uniform to unravel.

Tzoquito was still squirming. He couldn't stop; it was instinct now. You don't hold down a creature from the jungle. Not for any reason.

"Get off!" he was shouting in his own Mexican language for everyone in town and forest to hear. "Stop! Leave me alone! Eeeiiiiiii!"

"Christ! This one struggles like a wet cat!" complained one of the two unfortunate cops stuck with the task of holding him down.

Tzoquito repeated his shriek, this time louder.

"Eeeeeeiiiiiiiiyyyyyy!"

And louder still.

"EEEEEEEIIIIIIIYYYYYYY!"

Tzoquito shrieked over and over at this earsplitting volume. He got so loud that the cops, El É, Lupe and all the neighbors on all the balconies nearby had to put their hands to their ears to damp down the noise. The cop sitting on Tzoquito's back had to take his hands away to cover his ears and so he pressed down his head into Tzoquito's back to hold him down, his head now vibrating painfully with each bellowing shriek. But in any case, Tzoquito wasn't going anywhere now. He had stopped squirming: he was shrieking. And that was all he needed to do.

The sound of Tzoquito's voice was soon shaking the buildings of the town. People started running around on their roofs and terraces to see what was going on. There were shouts of "earthquake!" and *"Cállate!"* Shut up!

One neighbor looked up at the hills. She pointed to the hillside. "Look! It's a mudslide! He's causing a mudslide!"

Others followed her eyes. In the distance, dark shadows started spilling down from the trees of the forest. First like individual drops, then lumped together, like big black patches, moving toward the town. If it was a mudslide, this mud must have been alive. It was like nothing ever seen before.

"No, it's not!" said another neighbor. "It's the demons! That Tzoquito is calling them down to destroy us!" And indeed, swarms of black shadows descended on the town like a whirlwind. People came running from their houses, dust, papers and domestic pets flew through the air as a maelstrom of chaos took over. Impetuous black swarms invaded everywhere, blurring the world into cyclonic darkness. Up and sideways and down were all the same and people were thrown in every direction.

The cops were pulled up off of El É and Tzoquito and found themselves spinning around in the midst of the shapes. They could feel their arms being pulled, their legs twisting, their uniforms beginning to tear.

Tzoquito got up and pulled Lupe and El É to the shelter of an overhanging vine next to the house. The two human friends crouched down and hid their faces as Tzoquito crouched over them, protecting them from the whirl.

"What's going on?" Lupe asked in terror.

But El É was taking it all in stride. "That's your homeys, isn't it, Tzoquito? They came down to protect you."

"Yes, don't worry. They won't hurt anybody, not really. They just want to get the stones and bring them back to the forest."

Lupe looked out in wonder at the black swarms. "What a world!" she said.

El É whispered in her ear. "It's not so scary, though, once you begin to understand it."

Without thinking any further, Lupe grabbed El É's hand and pulled it close as she crouched further down. And the swarms of black continued to move in and out of all the houses, as though searching everywhere for something, sending people scurrying out onto the streets in the process.

A mass of black forms entered the burning chicken shed, putting out the flames. Finally, the whirling began to subside, all over town. But here at the chicken shed, it was more chaotic than ever, as though the swarms had finally found what they were looking for. Black forms converged from all sides and the three thugs shouted out as they went flying through the air, landing in trees farther down the street.

"Help! Get me down!" shouted Thug number three. "I'm afraid of heights!"

Jinete and Pinto, on the other hand, found themselves being pulled by both ears by some invisible forces, forcing them to weave their way up the street. They got dumped back into Jinete's garden, in pain but out of harm's way. They heard the garden gate slam behind them and they looked up in time to see the gate key turning in the lock and then the key flying up and away into the coiling sky.

The cops were still being spun around, barely seeing each other through the black swirl. Cop number one was getting sick to his stomach from all the spinning. He was going so fast that the rear end of his uniform pants were ripped off, revealing the Valentine pattern of his boxer shorts. He was let go and went rolling to the side of the street. He patted his butt, checking for something.

"Hey! Hey, you!" he shouted at the black swarms as they moved away. "Come back here with my wallet! You thieving demons!"

He ran down the street, chasing after the black shapes that were moving out of the houses one by one and disappearing in the distance.

"I had to take a little bite out of fifty cars on the state highway to earn the tips in that wallet! Give it back!"

But the black forms kept on going, sweeping down and out of the houses like a receding wave and moving swiftly out of town. The noise of these binquizacs began to die down, too and as the dust settled, the black swarms were being absorbed once again by the distant forest and the hills. The blue returned to the bowl of the sky like the blush on a baby's cheek, after the casual crying has stopped. A bird dared to chirp, just once.

With the air finally clear, the townspeople began to get up off the ground, or come out from hiding places or climb down from trees and precarious perches on the rooftops and ledges of buildings where they found themselves. With hardly a word, they got back to their feet in a daze, took some deep breaths of newly peaceful air and only then started moaning and cursing *"los perros encantados,"* the enchanted dogs.

In the new calm, three voices came through loud and clear. It was the three thugs calling out from the trees, begging to be helped down. Jinete and Pinto stumbled about in the locked garden, holding their twisted ears. Brolo ran up to them as they shouted out to him from behind Jinete's gate. "Find the key!" Pinto called, as he rattled the bars. "They locked us in!"

Brolo laughed. "Like common criminals! Don't you have a spare key for this gate?"

Jinete sneered. "Are you kidding? You think anybody's going to be able to find anything in this mess?" He pointed back at his aunt's house, where mattresses, tablecloths and furniture had been tossed up right to the windows. Jinete's aunt was just now standing in one of those windows, shouting abuse at her nephew and his good-for-nothing friends and banging a broomstick on the windowsill for emphasis.

"Hey," Brolo was amused. "Take your hands off your ears and listen to your aunt! She's talkin' to you!"

He tried to get them to show him the damage to their ears, but they were moody and uncooperative and wouldn't budge. They were holding onto their ears as though afraid they would fall off, so Brolo reached through the bars and pulled on Pinto's arm.

"Come on, man, let me see!" Brolo said.

"Shit! That hurt!" Pinto finally let Brolo see his ear.

"Hey! Now it matches your fat lip!"

"Why didn't they pull your ears, Brolo? You the one gonna let those thugs get away with the stones," Pinto pouted.

"Me? What're you talkin' about?" Brolo laughed. He was completely untouched. "Those dogs know a smart guy when they see one. My trick saved us from getting shot at. Shit, those *perritos* are smarter than you, *güey.*"

"Quit bullshitting, man" Jinete said simply. He was upset and embarrassed, though he didn't really know why.

"And you quit crying about your damn ears, man, there's nothing wrong with them. You just got spooked by a bunch of little dogs trying to teach you a lesson! You think they didn't see what you did to Tzoquito?"

He laughed but the others weren't amused. They were both ashamed for their actions the previous night, how they had betrayed Tzoquito and abandoned El É and now they felt like the whole world, even the demons in the forest, knew about it. So they stood there rubbing their ears and avoiding Brolo's gloating gaze.

"And they locked you up just to show you what you can expect from a life of crime!" Brolo finished with a sermon-like flourish, conveniently forgetting his own involvement in the affair.

Back in Lupe's garden, El É and Lupe got up from their crouching positions and just now realized that Tzoquito was no longer standing over them. They looked around the garden.

"Tzoquito!" Lupe called.

"Tzoquito!" El É called, too. He turned to Lupe. "He's not here. I'll go and look for him in the street. Why don't you go inside and check on your mother?"

Lupe jumped up and ran inside the house. "Mama! Where are you? Juanita! Miguel!" El É listened for a few moments, till he heard the sounds of a joyful reunion coming from inside the house. Then he went out to the road, where he was immediately taken aback by the sight of the four cops walking around disoriented and looking quite comical in their underwear. He had to hold back a laugh.

One of the cops pointed at him accusingly. "You shut up! This is all your fault! We should arrest you right now." Then cop number one looked down for a moment at himself in his underwear, remembering his missing wallet.

"Yeah, yeah! We're gonna arrest you!" he said distractedly as he walked around in circles inspecting the ground. Finally, a few steps away he bent down quickly and snatched something up off the ground. "Found it!" he shouted as he excitedly opened up his wallet. Then he let out a grown that turned into a shout. It was empty. He turned fiercely to El É and said. "That's it! We're going to arrest you right now!"

But the other cops were ready to move on. One of them was already getting back into the car. Cop Number One explained, "But we're going to let you go this time. We've got bigger fish to fry." He pulled up the remnants of his pants. "Real criminals! Not like you little guppies!"

The second cop stuffed the empty wallet into his belt for safe keeping and reluctantly got into the backseat with his colleague. "Come on, compadre," the other backseat cop called out. But Cop

Number One wasn't finished bragging, yet. "We just got a hot tip on the radio. We're goin' after some big time art thieves. And we're gonna catch them, too!"

"Yeah, you do that!" El É answered.

"Let's get out of this *pueblo de mierda!* This shitty town," the passenger cop said for the whole town to hear. "Fucking Indians and their damned demons! I'm never setting foot again in one of these loco towns as long as I live!"

When the cops were all in, the car set off with a screech, heading out of town, lurching wildly from speed bump to speed bump. El É was relieved that now he could turn his attention to other things. He was especially glad to see his three friends standing around down the street at Jinete's gate. He strolled grandly toward them.

"Hey, you guys!" he shouted. "You alright?"

"Yeah," Jinete said. Then he mumbled something else.

"What?" El É asked.

"I said, I'm sorry. For what I did to you last night."

"You should be apologizing to Tzoquito for what you did to him. You put him in a shitload of danger with that bag of dope."

"It was just a sugar cube, El É, but yeah, you're right. I've been acting very uncool lately. And then to top it off, we kind of panicked and left you guys behind."

"Yeah, I noticed," El É answered, somewhat sarcastically, but just a little bit. "But I only noticed about a half hour later, when I got a chance to stop running and catch my breath."

"You sure got back here fast," Brolo said. "Faster than us! How'd you do that?"

"You gotta ask Tzoquito, man," El É answered proudly. He's the man with the bag of tricks!" He looked in at Jinete's driveway, where the car should have been. "Yo, Jinete, where's my car?"

"Forget your car. First it burnt up, then your *amiguitos* ripped it to pieces looking for the stones. *Pinche perritos del Diablo!*"

El É looked with dismay at the mess in the next door neighbor's barnyard, where splintered wood, chicken feathers and smoldering car parts littered every square foot.

"Yeah, man," Pinto chimed in, squeaking back to life. "They took every one of those damned stones! They left us with nothing! With less than before! But that's fine with me! I ain't messin' with any of this shit anymore. You can keep your life of crime!"

El É smacked himself in the forehead. "They destroyed my antique Chevy!"

"Left it in a hundred pieces," Jinete said, not entirely displeased about it. "Probably did it just to punish you. Who do they think they are, anyway? Judge, jury and executioner."

El É shook his head. "Man! Now we're really stuck here!"

"Uh-uh," Pinto said. "Maybe you are stuck here. But we are getting the hell out of here, going back to *Califas,* if we have to hitchhike the whole way!"

"That's right man," Jinete said, picking up on the accusatory tone and passing it on, as though El É were personally responsible for this reprehensible place. "I ain't spending one more night in this town. You can keep the enchanted forest and your *cholos*. And that stupid art heist. This gangsta life is turning me into someone I ain't, someone greedy and mean and I don't go for that. We could have ended up in jail for life, do you realize that? I'm going back to my girl in Torrance. and my stupid little job!"

"Yo, man, I ain't going back to L.A.," Pinto said. "I'm sick of people pulling guns and shooting at me. I could get killed that way! I'm gonna join the U.S. Army and get away from all this!"

Jinete and Pinto slapped low five to each other.

"It doesn't look like you're going anywhere, till the *perritos* come back with the key!" El É said, just to dampen their style. Then he turned to Brolo.

Brolo held out his hand to shake. "Yo, El É, be cool. Thanks for everything." He seemed determined to strike a completely different tone from the others. "You know something, man? You're a real leader. Without you, I don't think we would have gotten past Mexicali, much less through all these things."

"So what does that mean? Are you leaving now, too?"

Brolo shrugged. "What can I do? I'm gonna go with them. I don't have anything here. I'll get back just in time to register for the new semester at community college. Maybe I'll stop on the way for some mud wrestling in Sonora. Just the usual stuff. But for you it's different, you have got a future here, you've got family and friends. You'll do fine."

El É nodded, not very enthusiastically. There were still a few wrinkles to work out with Lupe.

"And say goodbye to Tzoquito for me!" Brolo added. "That *perrito's* alright – *¡ese perrito es perron!"*

El É nodded again, this time with more energy and a smile. Then he looked around with a puzzled expression on his face.

"What's that horrible screaming?" El É asked.

"Oh, don't worry about that," Brolo answered casually. "That's just the sound of thugs crying in the trees. Just ignore it."

El É nodded, though he didn't quite understand. Thugs crying in the trees was not an image he had ever envisioned before – but neither was anything else he had seen in the past few hours. He waved at them and started walking away. He was anxious to get home and check how his mother had handled this whole affair. And come to think of it, now he had his own thoughts on magic that he would like to share with her. Like everyone else in Cielitos, he was still walking around in a half-daze, just now putting two and two together and becoming aware of everything very slowly. He was still getting feeling back in all his senses, like for instance, the feeling of a heavy lump in his pants pocket, as he headed home. He dug his hand in and pulled out a rusty metal object: the big iron key to a garden gate.

No point in wondering how it got there. He turned around and looked back up the street, wondering if he should bring it over and spring the detainees. He could hear them even from this distance, arguing with each other and with Jinete's aunt. She was now brandishing her broom in the air and shouting down at them furiously. Nah, he thought, let them enjoy some more quality family time together this evening. He preferred the peace and solitude of his own thoughts.

10

With all the changes in the world, one thing remained the same: the view from the ridge just above town at the edge of the forest. Tzoquito was there again just as in the old days and he was lying in his usual position, face on the rock, asleep. Eventually, the rays of the sun, as it lowered itself in the sky, awoke him.

"Sunset," Tzoquito whispered to himself contentedly, his eyes still shut. A cool rock, so familiar. His whole body and mind ached for something familiar and he gave in to it, with everything he had. He smiled and opened his mouth and stuck out his tongue to lick the cool rock, but his tongue was too short. Then he opened his eyes wider and sat up, suddenly aware of his human body and his history.

But not everything was immediately clear. The forest! How did he get up here? He crawled back toward the first bushes, on all fours, like the enchanted dog he secretly wished he could once again be.

"Tepiltzin!" he called out. "Tepiltzin!" he whispered. There was no need to shout.

A black form appeared under the bushes and its eyes twinkled in the shadows there.

"I knew it was you!" Tzoquito said. "You dragged me up here, didn't you."

"Yes and it wasn't easy, you have gotten a lot stronger than me, hombre! I'll have to grow human arms if I ever want to do that again."

Tzoquito fell back on the ground, with a laugh. It was so good to hear his brother's voice. "Thank you for being there for me, Tepiltzin!" But the words brought a shower of other thoughts crowding back into his mind. He held his aching head.

"Oh, I have to go back down there now and make sure that everything is alright."

"Don't worry about it," his brother said somewhat coldly, hurt that Tzoquito would think of leaving immediately. "Cielitos survived just fine before you went there and it will survive without you."

"But my friends!" Tzoquito protested. "And Don José and Abuelita, I have to see that they didn't get hurt."

"Don't worry! The binquizacs never hurt anyone! Have you forgotten even that?"

"I'm sorry. I didn't mean it that way." Life was getting complicated.

"You must really care about those terrible people. I can't understand that."

"I have changed, Tepiltzin. I am no longer that little pup. I feel new emotions. I feel joy. I understand a lot of things now that I never understood before. Before I knew not to hurt people but now I know why not. They are our cousins and they hold secrets inside themselves that belong to all of us. I knew that people loved and now I know how they do it."

"I envy you, Tzoquito," his brother said softly. "Your courage. I could never go down there and do that. I could never defy papa that way."

It was a wonderful compliment coming from his older brother. A compliment and an admonition at the same time.

It gave Tzoquito the courage to ask a favor, a very big one. "Please, Tepiltzin. Tell papa I'm sorry."

"You'll have to do that yourself, Tzoquito."

"Why? Is he here?" he said fearfully.

"No, Tzoquito, I came here all alone. Like everyday, everyday I have been here with you, Tzoquito. Learning along with you."

"And I have learned a lot, too" Tzoquito said proudly.

"Yes," his brother agreed.

"And not just about the many others. I have learned some things about the forest creatures, too."

"Really? What have you learned about us, my little brother?"

"I know how much you care about me, how much you love me, even though you don't know how. And I know that no matter how much you deny it, you all are as curious about the people in the valleys as I ever was."

Tepiltzin snorted his amusement. *"¡Eso es la verdad!"* he said, "That is the truth," in Spanish, a language Tzoquito had never heard his brother use before.

"You've been learning Spanish."

"Yes," Tepiltzin answered. "And it doesn't hurt, either. Not at all!"

"I told you that. But why are you learning Spanish?"

"I don't know. I've been learning it along with you. In case I ever need it."

"Need it for what?" Then a brave, new thought occurred to him. "Is it possible that you are planning to follow me?"

There was silence from Tepiltzin's side. Tzoquito continued with new excitement.

"Oh, yes, my brother, come out here with me!

More silence.

"Come on, Tepiltzin! Don José and Abuelita will help you, just like they helped me. If I can do it, you can too. We can do it together!"

Silently and slowly, a small hairy paw became visible under the bush. So much smaller and more fragile than Tzoquito remembered it. Tzoquito took that paw into his hand and he pulled. Slowly, in his grip the paw became more humanlike and it gradually became a hand. And then an arm emerged and another hand clasped on.

Tepiltzin's head emerged. It was like a miracle. To be sure, it *was* a miracle, but an exceptionally easy one, one that his brother's body gave in to as though giving in to the most cherished wish of nature itself. He was a young man, a bit older than Tzoquito, a perfect human being. His hair was matted and his upper chest scrawny and naked, but to Tzoquito he was beautiful. Tzoquito fell back in wonder.

"Tepiltzin! I can't believe it!" he gasped and tears came to his eyes.

"It feels so strange, but it feels good!" his brother said. They both laughed. Tzoquito finally heard his brother laugh.

"It feels so comfortable!" the older brother said, in a newly crafted voice, as he moved his arms around, flexing his new strength. "Now I know why you were planning to stay!"

"Were planning to stay? But I am still planning to stay, Tepiltzin. And now you'll stay with me!"

Tepiltzin got serious again.

"But I can't stay. I only came here on a mission. We can't stay, Tzoquito, neither of us. It's father's rule."

TEPILTZIN

Tzoquito was puzzled, as his brother took a few steps closer and embraced him with his newly formed arms.

And life continued to unfold surprises for Tzoquito, as all the marvelous joy he had experienced in Cielitos now suddenly paled in comparison to this new joy that he felt with his brother's tender human arms holding him close. He surrendered to his embrace. His brother had always been strong, much stronger than Tzoquito and even now, with his new formed muscles, his grip was tight. And tighter. And his arms wrapped around Tzoquito's torso with such strength, his hands pressed into him with his thumbs anchored so securely, that Tzoquito instinctively began to squirm to try to break free.

And then Tzoquito squirmed more and squirmed even more, but it was too late. Tepiltzin pulled him back and back and back, stumbling toward the bush. And then they were moving down, tumbling and shrinking down as they fell into the darkness. Then suddenly they both disappeared in a flash under the bush, shrinking into the black.

Tzoquito's human clothes went floating up into the air from the violent motion and when they inevitably fell, they came down to rest in a lifeless heap on the forest floor.

And thus, the sun set once again on Cielitos.

Early the next morning, two figures walked up to the home of Don José and his wife. It was Lupe and El É. They knocked on the open door.

"¡*Buenos Días!* Don José! Abuelita!" Lupe called in.

They were surprised when Don José's voice came up behind them.

"Hey, good morning, *mi hija!*" he said to Lupe. He didn't say anything to El É.

"Good morning!" she replied. Then she looked at El É.

"Good morning, Don José," he said and Don José nodded at him. "We came to make sure you and Abuelita were alright."

Now Don José smiled. He could only be severe for the shortest of times. "Yes, of course! We're fine. The *perritos* don't scare us!"

"And also, to see if Tzoquito was here."

Now the smile turned down. "No, he's not. And I don't think he will be back, either."

"He won't?" Lupe said with concern.

"No. I have a feeling the *perritos* took him back home where he belongs." He turned back to El É. "He hasn't been such a good boy since he met you."

"I'm sorry for the trouble I caused, Don José. I'll find a way to pay back the money he took. It was all my fault."

Don José laughed.

"Don't worry about the money, *joven*. Let me show you something."

He lead the two young people inside. Lupe was taken aback. The usually orderly house was in complete disarray. All the yarn pictures and nicely laid weavings that Abuelita was so proud of were scattered and ripped. On the floor was a crunching minefield of broken crockery, papers and clothing.

"Those binquizacs sure do make a mess!" Don José explained. "I'm still pulling my chickens out of the trees. But the forest creatures don't mean any harm, they're just very clumsy, that's all."

He picked up something from the table and held it out for El É to see.

"But they can be neat when they want to be. Look at what they left for me on the table, in one neat pile."

He was showing them a stack of banknotes.

"All the money that was taken! They gave it all back to me, down to the last peso! And they set it down under these."

He picked up four shiny metal discs and handed them to El É.

"What are they, *joven?*"

El É read the inscription. "*Estado de Chiapas.*" Then he looked up at Lupe and at Don José and smiled. "These are... I don't know how to say it in Spanish. *Badges. Policemen's badges.*" He said the last two words in English.

Don José snorted and repeated the word in English, the first time that Lupe or El É ever heard him use this language. "Badges?" His accent made El É smile in spite of himself. "*Placas de policía.* Why did they give us badges?"

"I don't know," El É replied. "We don't need no stinkin' badges!" he said in English with his funniest Mexican accent. But the joke was lost on his listeners, so he continued. "But the cooperative does need the money!"

That, at least, made them laugh. Don José laid the banknotes into the wooden money box and stashed it back under the bed. "Now you don't want to stay here in this mess," he said. "Go outside and say hello to Abuelita."

The two young people gladly obeyed and moved out of the messy house. El É saw that Don José's pig fence was crooked and needed some work.

"Do you want some help with that?" he asked and when Don José nodded, they set off to work straightening it out.

Lupe found Abuelita repotting herbs and inspecting the planters in her vegetable garden. She walked over to the elderly woman and said hello.

"Hello, *mi linda,*" Abuelita answered. "Is your mother alright?"

"Yes, thank you. Everyone is fine."

"I'm glad to hear that."

Lupe was just beginning to realize that this long living couple knew more than she had ever imagined. And so, after a hesitation, she asked a question. "Abuelita, do you think that Tzoquito will ever come back?"

"I don't think so, sweetheart. It is always the same with them. They always disappear again, just as suddenly as they came. This is not his world. He belongs somewhere else. That is just the way it is."

"I can't let him go like that, without even a goodbye. I have to talk to him." In reality, she didn't know what it was that she had to say, but she did know that she had to talk.

"Then talk. Maybe he's up there, listening right now." She looked up at Lupe and continued more confidentially, though there were no humans about to overhear them.

"That's the one thing I never liked about those enchanted ones. They're too curious. And nosy!"

Lupe looked up at the mountain.

"Abuelita, let's make some empanadas, like the ones Tzoquito likes so much."

164

Abuelita smiled and lead Lupe back into the house. "Alright, but we'll have to find the pots and pans first!"

The two men kept busy, too. It turned out that there were many things to fix in the fields and in the barn. The binquizacs had gotten into everything, it seemed. Three hours passed before El É and Don José came back to the house door, wiping the perspiration from their faces. Abuelita was on the porch now at her chores, alone.

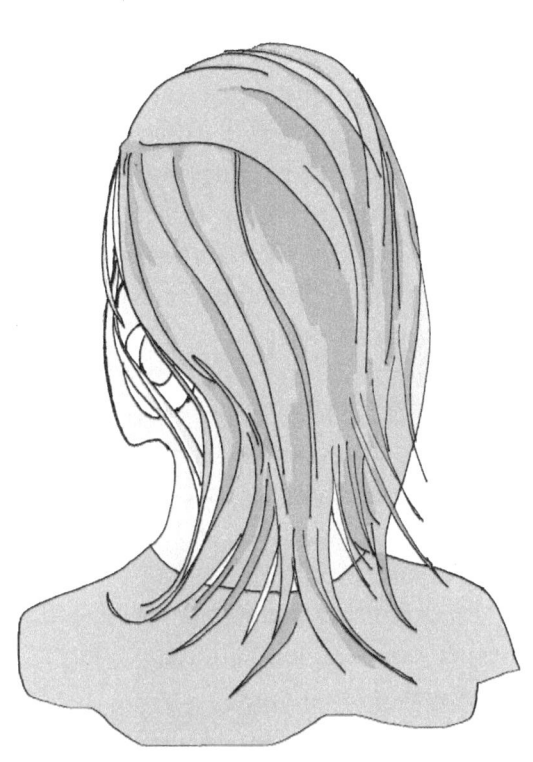

"Abuelita, where is Lupe?" El É asked.

She looked at him sadly and nodded in the direction of the mountainside forest.

"Where? In the forest? Doing what?"

"She went to find Tzoquito, about an hour ago."

"Find Tzoquito? Is she crazy?" He went back out a few steps down the path and looked up at the hillside. "Lupe!" he shouted. Then he ran a few more steps in that direction, but stopped. "No," he said. "I guess she will find her way back home by herself." He backed away slowly.

He sat down and ate the simple lunch that Abuelita had prepared for them, without really tasting it. Then he got up and took one last look at the hillside. He turned to these kind people and said goodbye. *"Adios, Abuelita. Adios, Don José."*

And he left, dejected, toward home, suddenly not knowing where he would go from here.

Another creature found that ridge that day, just hours after Tzoquito's encounter with Tepiltzin. Lupe knew this place, because Tzoquito had pointed it out to her from the road in front of her house. Now she came hurrying to it, a place she hadn't been to since she was a little girl, on a trek with her mother and father. And now she really did feel like a little girl, a girl in one of those fairy tales carrying goodies through the woods. In her hands she held a plate covered with a towel.

"Tzoquito!"

She called out a couple more times as she entered the trees and underbrush. She stopped a few feet into the shade, where she saw something familiar. It was Tzoquito's clothes in a heap. She sat down on the forest floor and touched the lifeless clothing wondering what to make of it all.

"Tzoquito! It's me," she said, in a conversational tone. She knew that this would be loud enough. "Please come out and talk to me!"

But there was silence.

"I brought you Abuelita's empanadas. Please, Tzoquito."

More silence.

"Tzoquito, I'm not leaving till you come and speak to me! Tzoquito!"

And when there was still no answer, she began to sob, slumping down further and further till she was lying on the soft bed of Tzoquito's abandoned clothing.

Dreams, strange dreams came to her in that green, botanical, intensely biological setting. But later, she would remember none of it. It was like voices in a foreign tongue, or like the images that swim before a blind woman who can suddenly see for the first time. She understood none of it. Nevertheless, it all seeped into her; it was all absorbed into her soul, thrilling her to the core. So much so, that she awoke from those exotic dreams exhausted and confused.

The sun was already low in the sky and its rays peeked in at her between the leaves. She was startled by a sound, a rustle from the forest but seeming to be right next to her. She turned around but saw nothing.

"Tzoquito!" she whispered. "Tzoquito, is that you?"

"Yes," came the answer in a soft garble. It was the way his voice had sounded that first night in the park in San Cristóbal.

"Where are you?" she said, jumping to her feet and turning every which way to see. It wasn't until the third turn around that she noticed the deep, dark shadow that had filled the area under the shrub next to her. She jumped in fright.

"Oh!" she gasped involuntarily.

"Don't be afraid, Lupe. It's just me. The real me."

She sat back down next to the blackness. "I'm not afraid, Tzoquito." And then as though to prove that it was true, she bent down low and put her face near the bush. The black shadow suddenly receded. And disappeared.

"What are you doing, Lupe?!" came Tzoquito's startled reaction, a bit farther away this time.

"I want to see the real you, Tzoquito. Let me see the real you."

Slowly the black shadow returned and filled in the space under the twiggy branches. Lupe peered in, eyes wide and full of courage. But she couldn't stay there for long. She pulled back suddenly and hid her face with a shudder.

"I didn't want you to look, Lupe. But I guess it's better that you did. Do you see, now? Do you see how ugly I am?"

She spoke through her crowded hands. "You're not ugly, Tzoquito. I was just surprised, that's all." She took her hands away from her face and bent down again. She looked in at the black shadow, without flinching this time.

"You are beautiful now," she said. "You are you."

"Yes, this is me and this is where I'm going to have to stay. Goodbye, Lupe."

"No, Tzoquito! Don't go! Don't leave me behind." She didn't know why she said this. It hadn't occurred to her, not before today's dreams, at least.

"Leave you behind? It is me that's left behind, Lupe, not you. You have the future there in Cielitos, you have everything ahead of you: the colors, the fantasies, the laughter of your world."

"But I don't want it, any of it! I just want to be with you, here in the forest, in a peaceful land."

Yes, in fact, it was the dreams. And now she was saying it and she would not stop. "No drugs, no *cholos,* no idiots of any kind. Please, Tzoquito, take me with you."

"¡No seas tonta, Lupe! You have your life in Cielitos. Human life that we in the forest can only imagine. You have people who love you there."

"Don't you love me, too, Tzoquito?"

"Of course, I do. But from a distance, Lupe, a distance of time and space and history."

"Once you told me that you figured out the reason why you came to Cielitos," she spoke with a voice moist with sorrow. "It was to meet me. Were you lying, Tzoquito?"

"No, I wasn't lying, Lupe. Meeting you was the greatest thing for me, because those feelings and those powers that you gave me are a precious gift that I am able to bring back here, to my home, to my.. " he hesitated for a moment, to find the word, to form the word on his tiring tongue. "... to my *people* here in the forest. We have a lot to learn and a lot to remember. Maybe then we can rebuild our own lives up here and we won't have to be so jealous of the people down in the towns anymore."

"And I can help you to do that," she insisted. "Please take my hand! Please take me in!"

Lupe extended her hand under the bush, but the black shadow once again receded.

"Please, Tzoquito, I beg you!"

Slowly, the black shadow returned. Lupe watched with a mixed thrill as a small, dark, hairy paw emerged and rested, palm up, next to hers, without touching.

Without a word she put her hand in his, but nothing happened.

"You must hold onto my motherless paw, Lupe, I have no thumb to grasp you."

And closing her eyes, she squeezed her hand tightly around his. Suddenly she was being pulled in. Pulled in! But after just a few inches, she let go with a jerk and freed herself from Tzoquito's paw.

"*¡Ay, Dios!*" the words escaped her in a gasp.

"What happened, Lupe?" Tzoquito asked with concern.

"I'm sorry, Tzoquito. I just got a fright, that's all. It was a mistake that's all. Let's try again."

Lupe put her hand back in position, but the black shadow suddenly receded again, farther back under the bush.

"No, it wasn't a mistake, Lupe. It was the truth."

"What do you mean? I'm ready now, Tzoquito, I'll hold on tight. Pull again!"

"No, Lupe. The mistake was for me to even consider pulling you into this place. You must stay there and live the things you learn in Cielitos, not here in the trees."

"I want to come to you, Tzoquito."

"Don't you see? It's the stones that want you to come. They have put these thoughts in your mind and made you believe. But your spirit says no. And your spirit makes the right decision."

His words made sense. She waited for him to speak more.

"Go back to Cielitos, Lupe. Go back to El É. He is the one who needs you."

Now she was completely confused – lost and in despair. "But I don't want El É, Tzoquito. I want someone different from that!"

"El É has changed, Lupe. Haven't you seen that?"

"Yes, he has," she had to admit this.

"He is ready to be someone different. And you will have to help him do that."

Once again she remained silent and waited for him to continue.

"Goodbye, Lupe, *mi corazón.*"

The black shadow disappeared and Lupe was left holding her head in sorrow. She sat there for a long time after that, not thinking about anything.

The sun was very low now. In fact, it had completely disappeared behind the mountains and now the darkness was seeping up, saturating the land, from Cielitos upward. Up from that gathering darkness, another creature now found this ridge, the one that Abuelita had indicated to him. El É came bounding up the hill, calling Lupe's name.

"Lupe! Where are you? It's getting late."

Lupe watched him from behind some tall grass. He went this way and that, calling her name and she watched like a cautious forest creature nestled in among the stones.

"Lupe! Lupe!" he shouted. He sat down against a tree and breathed in deep. "Lupe!" he said more softly now, with a despair that matched her own.

The softness of that voice now reached her in a special way. She looked at him with new affection and willfully broke out of her trance. She came out from behind the stalks and let herself be seen.

"I'm over here, El É"

El É jumped to his feet and came running toward her, agilely bounding through the vegetation, using a talent he had so recently acquired. She took a few steps back into the brush as he approached, pulled as though by magnetic force, the last weakened pull of the forest stones. She slumped back down onto the ground to wait for him to arrive.

"What the heck are you doing sitting in the woods?"

He looked down and saw Tzoquito's clothing on the ground next to Lupe. He came close and sat down beside her. He picked up the clothes curiously.

"Where is he?"

"He went back. I tried to go with him but I hesitated. I couldn't do it."

"Go with him, are you crazy, girl?" he laughed and put his arm around her. "You can't go there, you belong here. This is your home."

"I didn't want him to leave me. You can hate me, if you want, for being untrue, but that's it."

LUPE IN THE JUNGLE

"I'll never hate you Lupe, for being yourself. I know how you feel, you loved Tzoquito. How could you not love him? You're a real woman of Chiapas, as real as the soil beneath us. *¡Pura azteca!"*

"El É, we're more like Mayan, not Azteca."

"You see? That's exactly what I mean, you know all about these things. You've got it all under control! If I can learn to be a righteous Mexican with anyone, it will be with you."

Lupe laughed.!" What silliness, she said with affection.

"Tonterías que sean, but they are *tonterías* that can touch your soul, if you let them. Lupe, let them touch your soul."

He stroked her hair.

"And your heart," he continued and kissed her head. "I know I wasn't always honest with you. We came here with stupid ideas, me and my friends. We were going to make some money by stealing something. Something we had no right to even touch, much less take for our own profit. We were doing it just to make money and get some cheap respect from people who don't even matter. I want to make you forget all that. I want to make you forget right away, from today on."

He stopped to hear her speak. But although she open her mouth, no words came out. She simply rested her head on his shoulder and waited for him to go on.

"Come on, Lupe. Let's go home now."

"I can't! I can't leave Tzoquito here," she eventually managed to say.

"Lupe, you don't need to leave Tzoquito. We can take him with us, in our hearts, in our love for each other."

He gently kissed her on the lips, for the first time. Then as the stones finally lost their grip, he helped her to her feet and lead her out from the underbrush. They started down the hill toward the valley of the people, descending into the peaceful human night, where they would dream their people's dream.

After a few steps Lupe turned back and called out.

"¡Adiós, Tzoquito!"

"¡Adiós!" El É called too.

They turn back around and continued walking. Suddenly a voice was heard around their ears. It came from everywhere, the hills, the town, the trees and the sky but softer, as though it was made from the very breeze. It was Tzoquito speaking to them in his own tongue.

"Goodbye!"

Lupe and El É were startled, hearing that voice right next to them. They turned back all about, not knowing where to look. Then with big smiles on their faces, they called out wordlessly: Lupe calling into the dark, green woods and El É calling up to the just starry sky, in the silent language of their own understanding.

Goodbye, Tzoquito!

~~~~~

TZOQUITO'S
SPANISH AND MEXICAN
GLOSSARY

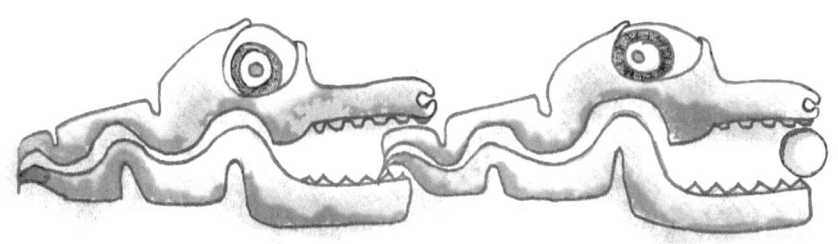

abuelita – Spanish diminutive term for grandmother (*abuela*).

amiguitos – little friends.

¡Ay, Dios mio! – Oh, my God!

Bacanora mezcal – a traditional alcoholic drink of the state of Sonora. It is made from the agave plant which grows in this mountainous region.

bebé – baby.

bebecito – little baby.

bien cholando – nonsense slang term giving the idea of a cool operation.

binquizac – according to legend, a group of indigenous people who could not bear to be subjugated by the Spanish conquistadors. They fled to the forest and there they were forced by the harsh conditions to transform themselves into forest animals in order to survive.

Bochil – a town in Chiapas. Federal Highway 195 runs through Bochil to the state capital at Tuxtla Gutiérez. Bochil is inhabited by people of the Tzotzil indigenous group. The Tzotzil, the largest ethnic group in Chiapas, is of Mayan origin.

cabrón – this term means a billy goat. However, that does not give an idea of its power as a curse word. It is used much like bitch or bastard in English and can also mean a cuckold, probably because a goat has horns, (*cornudo*).

Califas – Mexican American slang for California.

cállate, güey – Shut up, fool! *Güey* is a slang word meaning a dumb ox.

carreterra – highway.

el castellano – The Spanish national language. During the Fifteenth Century, the kingdom of Castile, with its capital at Madrid, became dominant in Spain and its dialect, i.e., *el Castellano*, became the national standard.

Cervantes – Miguel de Cervantes Saavedra (1547-1616), the author of *Don Quixote*, is the most famous Spanish writer in history. His influence on the Spanish language brings comparisons with Shakespeare in English. He died on April 23, 1616, the same day as the death of William Shakespeare.

chango – in this context, a monkey. The word can also refer to Shango, a *santería* god.

Chiapas – a state of southern Mexico with a Pacific coast and a border with Guatemala. Several famous Mayan archeological sites are located in Chiapas, among them Palenque and Bonampak.

chico – boy.

¡Chinga a tu madre! – an exceptionally rude expression. This verb *chingar* refers to having sex.

chingón – the word is a form of the vulgar verb meaning to have sex. This word is meant in a positive sense to mean something fantastic or very cool, but considering its origins, fantastic in a somewhat transgressive sense.

cholos – the term has been used historically to mean people of mixed indigenous and European race. It retains this meaning in certain parts of South America. In Mexican-American culture, the term refers to a type of person belonging ot a very specific subculture. The image of a *cholo* is a male Mexican-American who dresses in a certain hip-hop style and assumes a "gangsta" attitude.

colonia – colony in Spanish, it can mean a small community or village.

¿Cómo? – What did you say?

¿Cómo te llamas? – What's your name?

conquistadores – the explorers or conquerors who brought the Americas into the Spanish and Portuguese empires during the sixteenth century. The *conquistadores* are a chapter of Iberian and American history with an ambiguous feel and these men, for all their importance and impact, are not highly regarded on either side of the ocean.

¡Córrense de aquí! – Run away from here!

corrido – *correr* means to run, so *corrido* can mean many things. In this context, it is style of music: a Mexican ballad that relates the exploits of some colorful character.

desgraciado – despicable person.

¡Dime! – Tell me!

Distrito Federal, or D.F. – i.e., Mexico City. Founded as Tenochtitlan in 1325 A.D. (according to Aztec records), this city was destroyed by the troops of Hernan Cortes in 1521 and rebuilt a few years later. It became the capital of Nueva España and was the premier city of the Americas through the Eighteenth Century.

drogas – drugs

emigrantes – emigrants

Emiliano Zapata – 1879-1919. The most famous leader of the Mexican Revolution. He led Southern Mexican peasants in their demand for land reform during the dictatorship of Porfirio Diaz.

encantado – "enchanted," it is the most common formulaic way of acknowledging meeting someone for the first time (equivalent to English: "Pleased to meet you.")

ese pendejo – That idiot. *Pendejo* literally refers to pubic hair.

¡Eso es la verdad! - That's the truth.

Estado de Sonora – one of the 31 states of Mexico, located along the coast on the Sea of Cortes, (Gulf of California) the body of water between Mexico proper and Baja California.

los federales – the federal police.

flojos – lazy people.

flor de calabaza soup – Zucchini flowers can be used in several Mexican dishes. They may be stuffed with cheese or mixed with other vegetables. One popular use is as the main ingredient of soup.

güey – a form of the word *buey*, which means ox. Calling someone güey in the strictest sense means calling them a dumb ox, however, it is widely used in very informal conversation to mean "dude" or "man."

guiso de carne – beef stew.

Hernán Cortés – the Spanish conqueror of Mexico. It is often said that there are no monuments to Hernán Cortés anywhere in Mexico, though this is not entirely true: there is a mountain pass named for him and a bust of him at the National History Museum in Mexico City and the monument to *mestizaje* (the mixing of bloods) in an obscure park, pictured here. The body of water called the Gulf of California in English is called the Sea of Cortés. In any case, he is not a local hero and is not considered a Mexican, though he is in many ways, the illegitimate father of Mexico. His unequal liaison with the indigenous woman Malinche is one of the primordial myths felt deep in the Mexican psyche.

hijo de puta – son of a bitch, more or less.

hola – hello.

hispanidad – this term refers to the worldwide community of people who share the Spanish language and the cultural elements that this language brings with it. It might be translated as "the Spanish-speaking world."

huipil – traditionally woven article of clothing for women in Meso America. It has a square form and is used as a blouse or as a dress. There are innumerable different styles of huipil since every community has its own distinctive styles for everyday use and for dress-up occasions.

¡Húyense! – Run for your life!

Ichtaca – Nahuatl name meaning "secret." In this story, it is Tzoquito's uncle's name. His uncle is a shaman who has taught him an important trick that eventually helps him to become human.

indio – native Mexican, indigenous person.

Jinete – Spanish word for "horseman." One well known type of *jinete* is the *picador*, a man on horseback in a traditional bullfight.

joven – young man, youth.

lana – slang term for money. *Lana* literally means wool.

lucha libre – wrestling. It is *libre* or "free" because it is not subject to the rules of Greco-Roman wrestling.

maleducado – badly educated, rude.

maricón – yet another rude word for an effeminate man.

masa – dough for making tortillas, tamales, etc.

Maya – the most famous pre-conquest culture of Meso America, the mayans still populate the region in and around the Yucatan Peninsula.

mentiras – lies.

Mexican (language) – The most common indigenous language in Mexico, Nahuatl, is sometimes called "Mexican" by its speakers. In this novel the language spoken by the community of Cielitos is called "Mexican" as a generic term for indigenous language.

mi corazón – my love. *Corazon* literally means heart.

mi linda – my pretty girl.

mi hija – literally, my daughter, it is a very common affectionate term of address for a young woman, sometimes even thought of as one word *mija*.

montañas – mountains.

mujer – woman.

Nahuatl – the language of the Aztec people. It was spread throughout Mexico by the expanding empire and thus, became spoken far beyond its ethnic origins. It is the largest indigenous language in Mexico, with over one and a half million speakers from many different tribes. There is a large range of dialects and some are mutually unintelligible.

niños – children.

¿No hablas español? – You don't speak Spanish?

¡No les oigo! – I can't hear you!

¡No seas tonta! – Don't be silly.

el Norte – the north. In this context it is used to mean the United States.

¿Oíste? – Did you hear that?

Olmec – One of the earliest civilizations in Mesoamerica. The word "Olmec" is an Aztec Nahuatl word meaning "rubber people" and it was used by the Aztecs many centuries later to describe the people of that region, referring to their use of this substance. It is known for its enormous sculptures of human heads and other artworks of jade and obsidian. The Olmecs disappeared around 400 B.C.

paleta – ice cream pop.

Pan American Highway – a string of connecting highways constituting a single route from the Arctic Circle in Alaska to the southern tip of Patagonia. It is more of a loose concept than a concrete reality, with several alternate routes and conflicting histories. It runs from either Circle or Deadhorse in Alaska for 16,000 miles, or possibly for 29,800 miles to either Port Montt in Chile or Ushuaia in Argentina. In Chiapas, at least, the route is clear: Federal Highway 190 through Tuxtla Gutiérrez to the Guatemala border.

patán – generally used to describe a boorish person, especially from the countryside. In Mayan mythology, Patán is one of twelve malevolent gods who persecute humans with their cruel and violent tricks. Tzoquito would be startled to find himself called this.

paraje – small village in the outlying areas of a municipality, in Chiapas.

payaso – clown.

pendejo – see *"ese pendejo"* above.

perro – dog.

perron – cool, awesome.

perrito – little dog.

pinche – an adjective meaning fucking or damn, though not as strong as the former.

pinto – a variant of the Spanish word meaning painted, it has come to mean piebald, or patchy color. Pinto horses are a combination of white and other colors, usually black or brown. They were favored by the Native Americans because their coloring was a form of camouflage.

poblano – small town resident, villager.

por favor – please.

Placas de policía – police badges.

¡Pura azteca! – 100% Aztec. El É's favorite expression is meant to denote something authentically Mexican. However, this simply reflect his Mexican-American perspective. The story is set in an area well south of the Aztec world.

puto – similar to *pato*, it refers to a male homosexual. This is the male form of the more common word *puta*, which means a prostitute.

¡que malasuerte! – What bad luck!

¿Qué te importa, cabrón? – What's it to you, fool?

¿Qué te pasa? – What's the matter?

¡Qué tonterías! – What foolishness!

¡Qué vergüenza! – What a shame.

¿Quién es? – Who is it?

quinceañera – fifteenth birthday party, for a girl. It is similar to a sweet sixteen party in the U.S. and often very elaborate.

la raza – "the race." This term is sometimes used in the Mexican American community to denote their ethnic and cultural entity.

Rey Misterio – the name originated by Miguel Angel Lopez Diaz, a top star of wrestling in Mexico during the 1970s-80s. His nephew, Oscar Guitiérez, also known as Rey Misterio, helped revive the popularity of wrestling in the 1990s with his flamboyant style and retro *misterio* mask.

San Cristóbal de las Casas – city in the state of Chiapas, known for its long history and colonial architecture. It was the epicenter of the Zapatista revolt of the 1990s.

shaman – traditional wielder of supernatural power in many tribal societies, such as medicine man, witch doctor, faith healer.

Snidely Whiplash – this character is not usually associated with Mexico, but with Canada. He is the villain nemesis of the Canadian Mountie, Dudley Do-right in a popular TV cartoon of the 1960s.

soldados – soldiers.

Son diablitos. – They are devils.

Son mis homeys. – They are my buddies.

Tabasco – state of Mexico, on the Caribbean coast. The area was home to the Olmecs and then the Mayas and was invaded by the Spanish in 1518. Hernàn Cortés' settlement of Santa Maria de la Victoria was their first beachhead on the American continent in 1519.

Tepiltzin – Nahuatl name meaning favorite son. In this novel, this is the name of Tzoquito's older brother, who is indeed the favored son.

terno de lujo – *Terno* simply means a suit of clothing or an ensemble of some sort made from the same fabric. It could be a man's three piece suit, or as in this case, a woman's decorative traditional dress. In Chiapas and other areas of Meso America, each native ethnic group has its own traditional festive outfit for women to wear on important occasions, called *de lujo* or luxury. In some areas it may be a long skirt and blouse of ruffles and in others it may be an exceptionally embroidered huipil.

Tonterías que sean. – Even if they are foolishness.

Tuxtla Guttiérrez – capital city of the state of Chiapas.

ustedes – you, plural.

Usumacinta River – the largest river in Mexico, it rises in the mountains of Guatemala and runs through the tropical forests of Chiapas into Tabasco to the Gulf of Mexico.

valiente – a real man.

vámonos – let's go.

vato – like other slang words used to mean "dude" "bad boy" "homie" "gangsta," etc., the exact meaning of *vato* is elusive. It is often used to describe a neighborhood character who is part of the street culture. Other words such as *cholo* and *pachuco* are more hard-edged.

Ven acá. – Come here.

¿Verdad? – Isn't it true?

¡Vete a la fregada! – Get the hell out of here!

Yaqui Valley – The Yaqui River flows through Sonora. This river and valley bear the name of the indigenous group that historically inhabited these lands, including the Sonoran Desert and up into Arizona. In Carlos Castaneda's "The Teachings of Don Juan," the shaman Don Juan is a Yaqui.

Zócalo – Main square of a Mexican town. The original Zócalo is in Mexico City.

CHIAPAS

www.ingramcontent.com/pod-product-compliance
Lightning Source LLC
Chambersburg PA
CBHW022111170626
46808CB00002B/690